THE

MESSENGER

A Special Agent Dylan Kane Thriller

Also by J. Robert Kennedy

THE
MESSENGER

A Special Agent Dylan Kane Thriller

J. ROBERT KENNEDY

UNDERMILL PRESS

Copyright ©2021 J. Robert Kennedy

ISBN: 9781990418570

First Edition

10 9 8 7 6 5 4 3 2 1

For "the eyes" that didn't make it,
and those still waiting for a promise to be kept.

THE
MESSENGER

A Special Agent Dylan Kane Thriller

"Let believers not take for friends and allies infidels instead of believers. Whoever does this shall have no relationship left with Allah– unless you but guard yourselves against them, taking precautions."

Koran 3:28

"We cannot allow Afghanistan to be another Saigon."

Representative Michael McCaul
House Foreign Affairs Committee meeting
May 18, 2021

PREFACE

America's response to 9/11 was swift, with members of the CIA's Special Activities Division inserted into Afghanistan only 15 days later. Tens of thousands of troops would follow, and eventually almost 800,000 tours would be served in the country.

With a renewed hope for their country's future, approximately 300,000 Afghan citizens risked their lives by working with America and its NATO allies over the course of almost twenty years, including tens of thousands of interpreters, over 300 of whom died alongside foreign forces.

And they all did it with the understanding that when we left, we would take them with us if they so desired.

A promise, as of this writing, yet to be kept.

Wakhan Corridor, Afghanistan

Something wasn't right. Dax Laurier could feel it in his bones. Three tours in this hellhole had taught him to listen to that inner voice, and right now, it was screaming at him to get the hell out of there. But this wasn't his mission. He was just a sergeant major. The captain was in charge. Garrick O'Donnell was a good man, but this was his first tour.

At least he was approaching the end of it, so had some experience. The worst was when they came in green, full of ideals, not understanding that you couldn't trust these people, no matter how many rotting smiles were in the room. They only liked you when you gave them something, and they never believed you could actually protect them. This was war, and America and its allies were the invaders.

He had concluded long ago they should have never come. They should have just bombed the shit out of the place, leveled anything the

Taliban or Al-Qaeda had touched, then told whoever was left that if they did it again, we'd be back.

But instead, the powers that be had wanted to create a democracy out of a country that had no concept of it nor any desire for it. And how many had died? 9/11 demanded a response, and he agreed with that response at the time. But that time had long passed. The only way this country could ever be kept secure would be if half a million troops were put within its borders, and they might never be able to leave. The locals they were there to protect would eventually turn against them like many already had. It was a no-win situation, and he had no desire or intention to die here in some shithole on the other side of the planet from where everyone he knew and loved lived.

And today, his Spidey senses were telling him something was off. The smiles of the elders were more forced than usual, their eyes darting about with minimal eye contact made. The body language was all wrong, yet O'Donnell didn't appear to pick up on it. He glanced at their translator, Harifal, a man he had dealt with many times, and they exchanged a look. There was no doubt he had sensed the same vibe.

Something was wrong, and if this turned into a firefight, some sort of coordinated ambush, they were screwed. There were only six of them and one Humvee with a mounted M134 minigun, which was anything but mini. A drone was monitoring the situation overhead and air support was less than ten minutes away, but a lot can happen in ten minutes. He adjusted the casual grip he held on his M4, moving his hand slightly to cover the safety.

He flicked it off.

Sitting on several rugs laid out on the dirt floor, Captain O'Donnell glanced up at him, making brief eye contact. Dax's eyes darted toward the door then back at his captain, and the man nodded slightly.

"I won't take any more of your time today, sir. With your permission, we'll return in one week with the supplies you asked for." O'Donnell rose and everyone else in the room scrambled to their feet, the Afghans clearly not pleased with the early departure. O'Donnell bowed then extended a hand as Harifal translated the pleasantries.

Dax headed for the exit, if it could be called that, pushing aside a rug hung over the frame in place of the door that had once sat here, long forgotten. He squinted into the glaring sunlight, his eyes adjusting as he took in the area. They were in a valley, which was always a tactical disadvantage. Their Humvee was only 30 yards from their position. It would protect them against small arms fire, but if they were facing anything truly heavy, they could be in deep shit quick.

One of the elders was still talking to O'Donnell, his voice rapid and excited, but not in a good way. Harifal was translating.

"He seems to really want you to stay a little while longer to have more tea so they can discuss future needs."

O'Donnell stepped out of the home and Dax lowered his voice. "Sir, something's not right. We need to get out of here now."

"Agreed."

Dax swirled a hand over his head and the four others on the team standing guard around the village center cautiously returned to the vehicle, well aware they were leaving early. Wary eyes were cast at the doorways, the rooftops, and the mountains hemming them in on two sides.

Corporal Crawford pointed toward the mountainside to the west. "I've got movement!" He dropped to a knee, raising his M4 and peering through the scope. "Three targets, all armed with AKs!"

"I've got movement to the east!" called Specialist Perkins.

"Everybody in the Humvee!" ordered O'Donnell, and the moment he reached for his radio, all hell broke loose.

Jafar lay prone at the cliff's edge, peering down at the houses below and to his left. The Americans were inside the Imam's home near the village center, meeting with the local leaders with the weekly offering of bribes. Four of the infidels were positioned outside, watching for any trouble, and he had no doubt expecting none. After all, this was a peaceful area. There hadn't been trouble here in years.

He followed the road that cut through the valley, coming to a stop just to the south of where the ambush was to take place in fifteen minutes. Behind him, the soldiers of Allah who would be carrying out the attack traveled past him, all at a crouch to avoid being spotted by the Americans below.

"They're early!" hissed someone behind him.

He adjusted his gaze and cursed as the Americans emerged from the meeting ahead of schedule. He glanced over his shoulder. "Can you get in position in time?"

"No, we have to hit them now."

He shook his head. "That goes against our agreement."

"Your agreement is of no concern of mine. I have my orders."

He sighed. It wasn't his call to make, and it was too late to back out. He returned to observing what was happening below and cursed. "If you're going to do something, you better do it now."

But the suggestion was unnecessary, the warriors already rushing past him, scrambling down the mountainside. Somebody shouted from below, and a moment later gunfire erupted.

Dax Laurier grabbed his captain by the vest and hauled him toward their Humvee as gunfire rained down on them from the hills above. Someone cried out to his left and his head spun to see Corporal Taz Perkins down.

"RPG!" cried Specialist Allen Speck to his right.

Dax threw himself over the captain, still on the radio, as the rocket-propelled grenade whined toward them. It slammed into the opposite side of the Humvee, the din of the impact nothing compared to the shock of the massive vehicle being shoved several feet, flinging them into the open, completely exposed.

Dax lay in the dirt, pain racking his body as his head reeled from a high-pitched sound that threatened to overwhelm him. He struggled to push through the fog, squeezing his eyes shut in an attempt to block out the cause. Finally, the noise subsided slightly, enough for him to hear the gunfire and shouts surrounding him. Somebody grabbed him, dragging him along the rough ground and he gasped in pain, his ribs afire. Whoever had him let go and he dropped back onto the dirt, his chest heaving. He reached up and pressed a hand against the pain,

6

relieving it somewhat as he forced his eyes open to take in the situation. Captain O'Donnell was on a knee beside him, firing up at the hillside. No one else was near them, which meant O'Donnell had been the one who had dragged him to safety.

"We're not going to last ten minutes!" shouted O'Donnell into his comms. "I've got five down including my interpreter, likely KIA, one wounded, and at least twenty hostiles closing in on our position! Just blow the shit out of anything more than ten meters from my position!" He returned fire as Dax rolled over onto his stomach then pushed to his knees. O'Donnell cursed, clearly not pleased with the reply from Command. "Screw the villagers! They're in on it! They set us up! I repeat, the villagers set us up!"

Dax unslung his M4 and opened fire at anything that moved on the hillside. He glanced at the Humvee. If it weren't for the smoke billowing from the far side, it appeared intact, but the RPG had done its job. There'd be no using it to escape. He smiled slightly as he took down one of the attackers, then fired again and another dropped. The distinctive sound of an AK-74 split through the din, small explosions of dirt and rock erupting in front of them as the shooter found his mark.

Dax lunged to his right, shoving O'Donnell out of the way, and cried out as he took a round to the shin. He drew his knee up and grabbed at the wound, wincing in agony as half a dozen gunmen poured into the village center. He rolled into a seated position, raising his weapon and flipping it over to full auto, then squeezed the trigger, sending controlled bursts toward the approaching enemy. Two went down, taking rounds to their stomachs as the rest dove out of the way.

O'Donnell growled. "Looks like we're on our own. Help won't be here for another eight minutes. They won't fire on the village without a visual on the target."

Dax didn't say anything as he continued to fire while more hostiles rushed into the village center from all directions. He jerked a thumb over his shoulder at the home where the meeting had been held. "Get your ass inside there, Captain, and hold a gun to one of the old men's heads. It might buy you the time you need."

O'Donnell opened fire at a new group entering from the opposite end of the village center, then glanced over his shoulder at the door only feet away. It was the only hope. If the double-crossing bastards were indeed in on it, then using them as human shields should work.

Yet O'Donnell wasn't moving.

"Sir, you have to go now, before it's too late!"

O'Donnell rose, firing his weapon wildly as he grabbed Dax by the back of his vest. "If I go, you go."

Dax didn't bother protesting. Instead, he raised his weapon and fired as O'Donnell dragged him. Someone screamed in pain as the butt of the M4 pounded his shoulder with each shot. The door frame revealed itself as he cleared it, and it wasn't until the scream echoed off the walls inside that he realized it was him. O'Donnell propped him up against the wall and relief swept over him from the peace that stillness brought.

"Can you cover the door?"

Dax managed a nod, switching out the mostly-spent mag for a fresh one as O'Donnell disappeared behind him. There were shouts and a single gunshot from an M4. Dax glanced over his shoulder and saw several of the elders cowering in a corner. O'Donnell grabbed the imam by the beard and hauled him to his feet. He slung his rifle and drew his sidearm, pressing the barrel against the back of the man's head. He pushed the old man toward the window at the front of the house, any glass that might have once fit inside the frame long gone, shutters and a threadbare curtain the only protection from the elements.

"I've got your imam! You come any closer and he's dead, you hear me?"

Dax slumped against the wall. He could barely breathe from the broken ribs, and the blood was flowing freely from his shattered shin. Help was still five minutes out, and that was air support. It might stop the attack, but unless he got medical attention soon, he'd be done for.

"We need a damned interpreter!" spat O'Donnell as the gunfire continued. He tore the curtain from the window and shoved the old man's face through it. He repositioned the weapon so that it was clearly visible, the barrel now pointed down at the top of the man's head. "If you come any closer, he's dead!"

No interpreter was needed for the response to be understood. At least half a dozen weapons opened up, several rounds finding the old man. He collapsed to the floor, dead, as hole after hole was torn through the mud and stone walls, shafts of light revealing the trajectories. O'Donnell stepped back from the wall, firing his Glock through the window, his fingers squeezing the trigger slower and slower as the enemy rounds slammed into his body.

Dax cursed as he readied his weapon for what was to come. He eyed the old man dead on the floor, the leader of this village, and shook his head. How could they have misread the situation so badly? The villagers might have known about the attack, but they clearly weren't involved if those outside were willing to kill the Imam. And with what the captain had said over the comms, these people might pay the price as if they were behind everything.

A shaft of light appeared in front of him on the opposite wall, and a split second later the round that had created it pierced his neck, eliminating the only person who knew the truth of what had happened here today.

Or at least what he thought was the truth.

Operations Center 2, CIA Headquarters

Langley, Virginia

National Clandestine Service Chief for the CIA, Leif Morrison, stood in one of the state-of-the-art operations centers located at CIA headquarters in Langley, Virginia, his hands on his hips as he stared at the massive wall of displays that arced across the front of the entire room. Drone footage from two different events were playing side by side. One he had seen before, though he couldn't remember in what context, the other was new, the timestamp indicating it was from yesterday.

He pointed to the new footage on the right. "Is this from the incident in the Wakhan Corridor yesterday?"

One of his top analyst supervisors, Chris Leroux, confirmed it. "Yes, sir. It's from a drone that was dispatched the moment the distress call was received. Six of our people plus an Afghan translator were ambushed during a scheduled meeting with the village elders. They

11

were able to put out the call, but they were all dead by the time support arrived. The captain in charge indicated he thought those he was meeting with were involved."

Morrison pointed at someone entering the frame, leaning over each of the bodies. "What's he doing?"

"We believe he's taking photos of each of our people."

And then it clicked, the context in which he had seen the first video. He glanced over to the left side of the displays, staring at the footage from six weeks ago. Another incident, again in Afghanistan, half a dozen troops ambushed and killed. Unfortunately, there was nothing unusual about that, but what was odd was what had happened next. Caught by a drone, someone came in and photographed the bodies immediately after the attack.

Something strange was going on. ISIS had been known to take video of their victims and post it on the Internet to recruit other nutbars to their cause, but his agency and others had been monitoring, and nothing had appeared on the usual sites or the Dark Web showing footage of any of their dead.

For whatever reason these pictures were being taken, it wasn't recruitment purposes. Something else was going on, and so far, no one had the foggiest of ideas as to what it could be, beyond that a pattern had already emerged. Small groups of soldiers going into areas considered friendly were being ambushed on their way out. This was the first time a group had been ambushed within the village they were visiting, and with the captain's radioed warning that he believed the villagers were involved, it changed the equation.

The man with the camera left the frame and Morrison turned to Leroux. "Do we have anything more on that guy?"

Leroux shook his head. "No. The drone stayed over the town, waiting for reinforcements to arrive."

"And when they got there, what did they find?"

"No hostiles, and the town was abandoned."

"And now?"

"Latest drone footage shows the town is reoccupied."

Morrison chewed his cheek for a moment. "So, correct me if I'm wrong, but what we're saying is we had a team go in for a scheduled meeting, it appears they were leaving early and got ambushed inside the town. Then, immediately after the attack, someone was taking photos of our people before we got there, and before we did, the villagers disappeared until after our recovery team left."

"Yes, sir," said Leroux.

Morrison eyed him. "And what does that famous gut of yours tell you?"

Leroux stared at the footage on the screen. "The photos can't be a coincidence. Everything fits the pattern except that the ambush happened inside the village."

"So why the change in their MO?"

"Our people were leaving early. That has to be it. The question is why? Captain O'Donnell indicated he thought the villagers were in on it. For him to say that in the heat of the moment, he had to have picked up on something during the meeting and called things off. The meeting was scheduled for another fifteen minutes. My guess is the hostiles were moving into position for an ambush outside of the village when they had to change their plans."

Sonya Tong, one of Leroux's senior analysts and second-in-command, turned in her chair. "But why not just abort the attack? They put a lot of innocent lives at risk."

Morrison leaned against one of the workstations and folded his arms. "They must have felt the reward outweighed the risks."

Leroux bit his lip. "We're assuming they weighed the risks. We've seen it before in countries like this where they value life differently, and we're also assuming that the hostiles and the villagers are on the same side."

Tong regarded him. "But if the villagers knew, doesn't that imply an association?"

Leroux jabbed a finger at the air between them. "Exactly. 'Implies.' It doesn't mean there was a *friendly* association. The Taliban could have come into the village earlier in the day, told them to play along or else."

Morrison shook his head. "No, that doesn't make sense."

Leroux's eyes narrowed, the young man not accustomed to being disagreed with. "What do you mean?"

"The meeting was scheduled. Whoever committed the attack knew about it. If we're assuming this is part of a pattern we detected, then they had plenty of time to set up their ambush outside of the village just like the others. There was no need to inform the villagers of anything. The meeting would happen, it would end amicably, our people would leave, and the hostiles would ambush them. There was no need to involve the village in any way."

14

Leroux's head bobbed. "You're right. So, if the villagers knew, then it certainly suggests they were either in on it, or had been informed for some reason. What that reason could be, I have no idea." He rubbed his chin with his thumb and forefinger. "Here's a crazy idea. We're assuming the hostiles were Taliban or some other group. What if they were from the village? Not an outside group like we've been thinking."

Morrison rose and stared at the screen, contemplating Leroux's theory. He wagged a finger at the display as he turned back. "That's an idea, that. This area was considered secure, and so were all the other ambush sites. Taliban activity has been minimal there."

Randy Child, the team's tech wunderkind, spun in his chair, staring at the ceiling. "I don't buy it. It takes some serious cajones to ambush seasoned troops. I can't see villagers doing that, at least not without some serious motivation. My money is on this being some new group."

Leroux regarded Child. "If it is, then why aren't they using the photos they've been taking for recruitment to their cause?"

Morrison sighed and returned to his perch on the edge of one of the workstations. "That's what I don't understand. If you want to recruit, there's no point posting all your material in some corner of the Dark Web that nobody knows about. We've been monitoring all the known haunts and haven't seen anything, which has to mean either the images they're taking are never meant to be made public, or they're saving them for something else down the road."

Tong shuddered in her chair. "What could that possibly be?"

Morrison shook his head. "I don't know, but we better find out. Otherwise, the dozens that are dead already may be merely the tip of the iceberg." He headed for the door. "Get an asset in the area. I want to know what the hell is going on before any more of our troops are slaughtered."

Outside Langley, Virginia

CIA Special Agent Dylan Kane downshifted then hammered on the gas, the 797-horsepower engine of the 6.2L Hemi V8-equipped Dodge Charger he was in slamming him into the back of his seat. He wanted to smile, though if he did, he'd be giving in to the adrenaline of the situation. He loved a good car chase, especially one that involved guns, but he had to focus.

His target was just ahead, and the chase had been on for almost ten minutes. He hadn't been able to overtake them yet, the target driver exceptionally skilled in an equally powerful vehicle. A sharp turn approached and he smiled as the back end of his opponent's car lost its grip by only a hair.

Yet it was enough.

Their speed was killed dramatically as the driver was forced to let up on the gas more than planned. He gunned his engine, ignoring the turn, instead punching his front bumper into his opponent's rear before hammering on the brakes, downshifting, and spinning the wheel, all in one fluid, choreographed moment. As he came out of the turn, his opponent's back end swinging in the wrong direction, he reached over and grabbed his weapon from the cup holder, extending it out his open window as the driver's side window of his opponent came into sight.

He smiled at the shocked face of his girlfriend, Lee Fang, as he squeezed the trigger, putting two in her chest then two in her face. Both cars screeched to a halt. He threw open his door and stepped out, striding over to Fang's vehicle, now perpendicular to the road. His smile spread as he confirmed the perfectly placed shots.

Suddenly, Fang's weapon appeared in the window and she fired twice, both hitting him square in the nuts. He dropped to the ground, writhing in agony, his gun clattering onto the pavement as she stepped out. He stared up at her as she aimed her weapon at his head.

"Hurts, doesn't it?"

He gripped the companions to his most favorite body part as tears filled his eyes. "Ya think?"

She pointed at the two bright green paintball splatters on her chest. "I hope so. It hurts getting shot in the boobs, you know."

He winced. "I don't think you can compare it."

She shrugged as she removed her helmet, the face shield smeared with paint. He rolled over onto his back as a golf cart with a rotating amber light arrived, the course marshal shaking his head with a smile then outright laughing at Kane's literally blue balls.

"Beautiful takedown, Dylan. You executed that PIT maneuver perfectly." He turned to Fang. "Ms. Lee, do you know what your error was?"

She fired two rounds into Kane's helmet then holstered her weapon. "I entered the corner too fast. It forced me to overcompensate when my back end kicked out. That allowed him to overtake me."

"Exactly. You never want to present a corner to your opponent like you did. You're better to slow up when your bumpers are square. That way he can't knock you out. Kill your speed, accelerate into your turn, and your opponent has to do the same."

Kane groaned as he rolled to his knees and removed his helmet. He pointed at his balls. "She should lose a few points for this."

The marshal eyed the region. "Looks like good grouping to me."

Kane flipped him the bird and the man shrugged.

"Hey, you're the one who wanted to play spy games with your girlfriend." He grabbed his moobs and gave them a lift. "And take it from a guy who knows, getting shot in these hurts."

Kane pointed at his balls. "More than this?"

The marshal shrugged. "No idea. I haven't been dumb enough to play paintball without a cup."

Kane gave him a look. "We were doing it inside cars. I didn't think I'd need it."

The man shrugged again. "There's no rule that says the game stops when someone gets out of their car."

"Yeah, but there is a rule that says it stops when you're dead."

Fang grinned. "Zombie Paintball Racing."

Kane pushed to his feet using Fang's car to steady himself. He hopped a couple of times to free up any of the boys that had revisited the home of their youth, then took a tentative step. They were tender, but he'd live.

Fang stepped over and patted his cheek. "Is my baby okay?"

"You should be asking *him* that." He cast his eyes downward.

She cupped his boys and gave them a squeeze. He grunted and winced. Her playful expression turned to concern. "I really did hurt you, didn't I?"

He gave her the eye, repeating his earlier question, this time more emphatically. "Ya think?"

She shrugged. "I wouldn't know. My body wasn't designed stupidly."

Kane eyed her. "You didn't seem to mind the design last night."

The marshal roared with laughter. "You two aren't married, are you?"

Kane shook his head. "No."

"You can tell."

Fang's eyes narrowed. "How?"

"Because if I shot my wife in her tatas, she'd have got out of the car, hoofed me in the balls several times, then walked away expressing absolutely no concern on whether I was okay."

Kane laughed. "She's a black belt to the nth degree. If she ever decided to kick me there, I'd be spitting out chestnuts." His CIA customized TAG Heuer watch sent a pulsed electrical signal into his wrist, indicating he had a message. He turned to Fang. "Well, my dear, I don't think we're going to do a second round today. I have to go ice these things before they become useless."

She stared at him. "I'm sorry. I thought you were wearing a cup. The game rules dictate the mandatory equipment."

He frowned at her. "You know me, I don't play by the rulebook."

"And that's why your balls will be blue for a few days." The marshal indicated both cars. "I assume they're still drivable?"

Kane glanced at the reinforced bumpers. "Oh yeah. I only gave her a love tap. I doubt there's even a scratch." He eyed the beat-up vehicles, then shrugged. "Well, I doubt there's a *new* scratch."

The marshal climbed back in his golf cart. "Then get them off the course. I've got people waiting."

Kane delivered a Sergeant Bilko salute. "Yes, sir!"

Fang giggled and they both got behind the wheels of their vehicles, following the marshal back to the pit. Kane pressed the buttons surrounding the watch face in a coded sequence, then tilted his wrist to read the message scrolling across the crystal, indicating he had a non-urgent message from Langley, specifically from his best friend, Chris Leroux. He sighed. This was his time off, but apparently Langley had other plans for him.

He shifted in his seat and delivered a silent apology to his testicles for what was to come.

Operations Center 2, CIA Headquarters
Langley, Virginia

Chris Leroux continued through the after-action reports and the investigation summaries into the previous half-dozen similar incidents, refamiliarizing himself with what had happened over the past couple of months. Six ambushes, all small groups in friendly territory, all hit after leaving their scheduled meeting, except for this latest. And this was the second one where aerial footage had caught someone taking photos.

Attacks like this had happened throughout the almost 20 years America had been in Afghanistan, and if it weren't for the reports of the photos being taken, nobody would be paying any more attention than they normally would. While the six previous attacks followed the same pattern, it could be nothing, it could be mere coincidence. But he didn't believe in coincidence.

And the cameramen changed everything.

He leaned back, folding his arms then scratching at his chin. This one outlier and the radio transmission received from the captain leading the mission spoke volumes. If this latest attack weren't an outlier, and instead was part of a pattern like he suspected, where the villagers were aware of what was about to happen but something had gone wrong, then it suggested that the same was true in all of the previous attacks.

But what would they gain? Part of America's policy in Afghanistan was to win the hearts and minds of the locals, and the most effective way to do that was through plain old bribery, primarily through supplies and infrastructure as opposed to greased palms. What could villagers possibly hope to gain that could outweigh America and its allies coming in and building a new school or digging a new well?

"Their lives," he muttered.

Tong turned in her chair. "What was that?"

He shook his head. "Nothing, just talking to myself." He turned so he was facing more of the room. "I was just thinking that if there *is* a pattern here, and this latest attack was conducted by the same people or at least people affiliated with each other, then it suggests all of the villagers knew that the attacks were going to happen. And if that's the case, they set our people up, but they would have to know that if we found out, any assistance we're providing them would be lost. So, what could the Taliban possibly offer these villagers that they'd be willing to give up everything we could offer them?"

Child shrugged. "Their lives, I guess, like you said. Cooperate or we'll kill you."

Tong shook her head. "That doesn't fit."

"Sure it does. These people are animals."

"Perhaps, but they're not stupid. Why would they tell the villagers anything? Like we've discussed before, there was no need. All the ambushes except for this one were set up outside of town."

Mark Therrien, one of the team's senior analysts, leaned forward. "They'd have to know when the meetings were happening, wouldn't they? I mean, these were well-coordinated ambushes. It's not something you can throw together on an hour's notice unless you already had people in the area."

Leroux agreed. "Yes, but these meetings are prearranged. Our people don't just show up in a village and ask to have a meeting. Not in these areas where we're trying to be courteous. Quite often, the locals will gather around the meeting place to hear what the news is, to find out what they were getting from us in exchange for their cooperation. All the Taliban would need is one sympathizer inside the village. He hears when the meeting is happening, passes the intel along, and then his cronies set up the ambush. No need to involve any of the villagers."

Therrien chewed his cheek for a moment. "Maybe the informant is one of the people in the meeting, or one of the people in the meeting was bribed."

Tong shook her head. "No, the Captain's transmission indicated he thought the villagers, *plural*, were involved. One informant or one traitor doesn't tell a room filled with community elders what they've done. He keeps it to himself. If the Captain's right and the villagers in the meeting knew, that suggests they discussed it among themselves."

Leroux's head bobbed slowly as he turned his chair to face Tong. "You could be on to something there. Somebody came to them with a proposal, they debated it, like any city council would, came to a decision to betray our people, and something happened that tipped our people off, and they ended the meeting early, triggering the improvised response."

"That fits. The question is, who came to them? At some of these ambush sites, the locals have been on friendly terms with us for a decade. I doubt the idea was cooked up by the locals." Tong threw up her hands. "The only way we're getting any answers is with boots on the ground."

Leroux agreed and checked his watch, wondering why Kane was taking so long to get back to him, then smiled slightly at the stupidity of his question. Kane hadn't seen Fang in weeks, and he had no doubt they were spending most of their time catching up rather than monitoring communications.

They might never hear from him unless the urgency code was escalated.

Kane/Lee Residence, Fairfax Towers
Falls Church, Virginia

Kane groaned in pleasure as he sat on the couch, knees spread wide, Fang on the floor in front of him, his eyes rolling back in his head. "That feels so good."

"I don't doubt it." She pressed the icepack against his balls. "I guess next time you'll wear a cup."

He gave her a look. "I guess next time you won't shoot me in the nuts."

She lifted her top off, revealing two welts on the twins.

He winced. "Ouch."

"Exactly, so we're even."

He shook his head. "No, we're definitely not even. But you're further away from zero than I thought you were." His watch pulsed again, the pattern indicating a higher level of urgency than the first time. He had assumed his buddy had used the covert method of communication so as not to disturb him if he happened to be getting familiar with his girlfriend. Ball ice was more important than reconfirming dinner plans the two couples had this evening, though this level of urgency couldn't be ignored. He tapped his watch, the electrical pulses undetectable to anyone but himself. "That would be Chris. Can you hand me my phone?"

With one hand still pressing the icepack in place, she reached behind her and grabbed his phone off the table then handed it to him. He logged in, then called his best friend, someone he first met in high school. Leroux was two years his junior, a brilliant loser that Kane's parents had hired to tutor him to keep his grades up high enough to stay on the football team. Kane was the stereotypical jock—popular, good-looking, successful with the ladies, without a care in the world. All he was concerned about was getting a football scholarship so he could go to college.

Leroux was brilliant, unpopular, teased relentlessly, and had never kissed a girl, his brilliant mind destined to help the world.

They were polar opposites.

The only thing they had in common was geography—they attended the same high school. Yet against all odds, they had become good friends, and he had protected Leroux from the bullies, giving the poor guy a brief reprieve.

They had gone their separate ways, neither realizing the other had ended up at the CIA until a chance encounter at Langley reunited them, and they had become close friends over the years, best of friends, both of them now living in the same apartment building with the women they loved.

He brought up the message confirming it was his friend, and that the urgency level had increased. It still wasn't indicated as critical, but there was no doubt now this was something that could no longer be put off. He tapped the link that would automatically encrypt and dial Leroux's station at Langley, and his friend answered on the first ring.

"You know I'm on vacation, right?"

Leroux chuckled. "Does a CIA operative ever actually get a vacation?"

He grunted. "I never really noticed until Fang and I started dating." She flashed him a grin then removed the icepack, giving things a kiss to make it all better. He wagged a finger, warning her not to start anything. Not only was he still in too much pain, he had a sense he was leaving shortly. "So, what's going on that has you zapping my wrist twice in the past hour while I'm off duty?"

"We've had a series of ambushes on our troops in Afghanistan over the past couple of months. All in normally peaceful areas, all small groups, all after meeting with local leaders."

Kane frowned. "I heard on the news this morning about another ambush yesterday. Six dead, I believe?"

"Seven, including the Afghan translator. And that's why I'm calling. You're heading back into the region in two days regardless, and your handler said she can spare you for this op, so…"

Kane flinched as the icepack was pressed back against the boys.

Fang rose. "I'll get your stuff ready. Region?"

"Afghanistan."

"Okay." She headed for the bedroom and he stared after her, her top still off, revealing her ripped physique. Dylan Jr. threatened to take a peek for himself and Kane gave him the evil eye.

"I take it there's more to this attack yesterday than what the press is revealing?" he said, returning his attention to where it should be.

"Yes. This one didn't fit the pattern. It happened inside the village where they were holding their meeting, and the captain leading the mission radioed in that he thought the locals were involved. What caught our eye was that after the ambush, we have drone footage of someone taking photos of the bodies."

"Recruitment photos?"

"Possibly, though nothing's shown up yet. But what you don't know is that six weeks ago, the exact same thing happened. A drone caught someone taking photos after an ambush, and they've never shown up anywhere."

Kane's eyes narrowed, his pain momentarily forgotten. "Wait a minute. If they weren't recruitment photos, what were they for?"

"We have no idea. That's why we want boots on the ground with good local connections. We're sending you in to find out what happened. This is the first time we've got intel that suggests the locals were in on the ambush, and that doesn't fit."

Kane's head bobbed. "There'd be no need to tell them, and why risk all the goodies we give them?"

"That's exactly what we're thinking."

"Okay, when am I leaving?"

"Arrangements are being made. How much time do you need?"

Kane glanced at the icepack. "I'll have to ask my balls."

"Huh?"

"Long story, buddy. I'll let Fang tell you tonight, and then you can tell me how much pleasure she appeared to take in it."

"Umm, okay."

Kane roared with laughter. "Don't worry, it's got nothing to do with sex."

"Oh, I see. Actually, I don't see. Dylan, I have no clue what the hell you're talking about. And there's no way in hell I'm asking your girlfriend about your balls."

Kane shrugged. "Your loss."

"I think I can live with that. So, when should I have them pick you up?"

"Give me thirty minutes."

"Good. Your Uber"—Kane could hear the air quotes—"will be there in thirty. The driver will have a detailed briefing package, at least as detailed as we can make it. We don't really know a lot at this point."

"What's your gut telling you?"

There was a pause, then Leroux finally sighed. "I'm not sure, but it's nothing good. Either there's a new player in the area that's collecting material for a recruiting blitz at some future point, or something's changed with the existing players, and we need to find out what, otherwise a lot more of our people could die."

Goosebumps rippled over his flesh as his friend's tone had his subconscious agreeing something was going on. You didn't stick around after an attack to take photos of the bodies then not use them. "Don't worry, buddy, we'll get to the bottom of this. Talk to you soon."

He ended the call, then waddled into the bedroom, pressing the icepack against his throbbing nether regions. He found Fang in the bedroom, a carry-on and a full-sized suitcase opened on the bed, half-filled with what any insurance investigator would require in a region known for its heat at this time of year.

She nodded toward the icepack. "How's the happy sack?"

He groaned as he flopped onto the clear side of the bed. "Not very happy at the moment."

She paused her packing. "Is it going to affect your mission?"

"I hope not. It's not like I can tell the Chief, 'Sorry boss, but my girlfriend shot me in the nuts and I can't go and save our country today.'"

She giggled and he gave her the stink eye. She covered her mouth with three fingers. "Sorry, I know you're in pain and I shouldn't laugh."

"No, you shouldn't."

Her eyebrows bobbed suggestively. "Anything I can do to take your mind off things?"

Fingers on both hands stabbed toward his wounded soldier. "Is he just a tool to you? Am I just the charging station?"

She regarded him, clearly puzzled.

He waved a hand, chuckling. "Just pack my bags for me, please. The longer I can ice these chestnuts, the better." He eyed the welts on her chest. "Are those as painful as they look?"

"Yes."

He pushed up on his elbows. "Then let me pack."

She dismissed his offer with a flick of a wrist. "Don't worry, I've got it. We women aren't wimps like you men."

Kane collapsed back on the sheets, surrendering to the female of the species, all the fight he normally had in him cowering in fear between his legs.

Istiklal Avenue

Istanbul, Turkey

Kane sipped his cup of Turkish coffee and suppressed the wince, as he had trained himself to do. He hated hot beverages, especially coffee. Tea was tolerable, depending on the type. In his personal life, anything hot rarely crossed his lips voluntarily, but on the job, with the majority of the planet enjoying their hot drinks, he couldn't be the odd man out, so he learned to feign enjoyment. He had assumed that over the years it would at least grow on him, but it never had.

Today, he could have made an exception and ordered a diet soda or a bottle of water, but he was in character now. The moment he boarded the flight to Istanbul, he was Dylan Kane, insurance investigator for Shaw's of London, and across from him sat his CIA handler, Beverly Thorn, appearing fully recovered, at least on the outside, from her recent ordeal.

"I was sure you were going to retire."

The woman, easily thirty years his senior, eyed him. "And here I thought you knew me."

Kane rolled his eyes. "Riiight, because you're always talking about your personal life."

She smiled. "I'll admit, after what happened, I considered it, but ultimately decided I didn't trust anyone else to manage your affairs. Besides, I'm fully recovered."

Kane smiled. "Well, I'm happy I don't have to break in a new handler, but I'd hate for you to delay your retirement just because of me."

She put down her cup of Turkish coffee—her favorite, not his—and wagged a finger at the waiter then indicated her cup, a refill arriving a moment later. She smiled at the young man as he retreated, then took a sip, lowering her voice slightly. "The files you requested have been sent to your secure account, along with your cover details. I arranged for you to have a meeting with the Afghan Urban Development and Housing Minister to discuss insuring some of their bigger projects against terrorist attacks."

Kane grunted. "Only a CIA front would ever issue those policies."

She smiled. "No one says you're going to sign anything. You're just there to discuss the possibility."

"Is he one of ours?"

She shook her head. "No, but he's friendly to the cause. Don't break cover, but I'm sure he's wise to the fact you're not there to actually see him, understood?"

"Got it."

"So, tell me, why did you request those files on the villages involved in the previous attacks?"

"Because, frankly, I don't expect to find much where the current attack happened."

Her eyebrows rose. "Oh, I would have thought the freshest intel would be at the latest site."

"Oh, I agree, and I'll be going there first, but we're looking for motive, right?"

"And what makes you think you'll find that at the older sites, as opposed to the newest?"

"If the elders of the village were involved, after so many years of being friendly, what changed? What did they have to gain? I agree with Leroux's team's assessment that it doesn't make sense for the elders to have been informed of the attack unless they were involved. There was no reason to threaten them to cooperate, because all they had to do was let the villagers hold their meeting as scheduled, then ambush our people outside of town just like the others. So, if we eliminate fear as the reason to cooperate, then there has to have been some sort of financial motivation."

"Perhaps they simply changed their loyalty."

"Perhaps, though that many in two months? And keep in mind, the other villages still welcome us with open arms."

"True, so what are you thinking?"

"I'm thinking that if there were some motivation to cooperate with the hostiles, they had to have gotten something out of it. I'm hoping the updates I requested might reveal just what that motivation was."

Her mouth slowly opened as her head bobbed. "Ahh, that's why you requested those new UAV overflights of all the villages. You're looking to see what changed."

"Exactly. If everything appears the same, outside of anything our forces did for them, then it suggests the villages involved in the previous attacks weren't involved at all. But if something's changed, if somebody has a fancy new house or a shiny new car, something out of place and expensive, then it suggests somebody was paid, and the site of the latest attack won't show any evidence of that because it's too soon."

Thorn grunted as her head slowly shook. "I love the way your mind works. You don't believe at all in the basic goodness of people. Everyone is out for themselves."

He shrugged. "Experience. It's not necessarily true everywhere, but it's certainly true where your every day is a constant struggle just to survive."

"Your plan is what?"

"I'll have your meeting to maintain my cover, but I'm meeting up with an old translator buddy of mine and we'll pay the various sites a visit. If my hunch is correct, there's going to be some uncomfortable questions that need to be answered."

Thorn finished her second cup then hailed the waiter, indicating with a scrawled air-signature for him to bring the check. Kane finished the last of his first, forcing it down, then popped a piece of gum in his mouth to rid himself of the unpleasant taste. He didn't bother offering a piece to Thorn, for it would be refused. The bill was brought out and she dropped a handful of lira on the table, the waiter beaming at the generous tip, thanking her repeatedly as he bowed his way out of their personal space.

Kane rose and extended a hand. Thorn took it, and for the first time ever, actually needed the support. She grimaced as she stood, and his chest ached with the knowledge she wasn't recovered after all. She drew a sharp breath then exhaled before she let go of his hand. They left the outdoor café and strolled along Istiklal Avenue.

"You lied to me," he said.

She glanced at him. "Did I?"

"You said you were fully recovered. You're not."

"I'm recovered enough."

"Does Langley know?"

She shook her head. "The doctor who did my assessment is an old friend."

Kane rolled his eyes. "That beating you took would kill most people your age."

"My age?"

He gave her a look. "You know what I mean?"

She chuckled. "Yes, I suppose I'm no spring chicken."

"And there's nothing wrong with that in most businesses, but what would you do if we were ambushed."

"Even healthy, there's not much I can do anymore."

"Bullshit. I read the reports of what happened in Helsinki, and there's no way you'd be able to do now what you did then in your current condition. More would have died."

She sighed. "You're right. But I owe you, and you need me."

He smiled down at her as they continued past Taksim Square. "I'll tell you what. Your secret is safe with me as long as you promise to cut out these meetings. You and I both know this could have been done over a secure line."

She frowned then finally nodded. "You're right, of course. No more meetings until I pass my physical."

"Good."

She pointed toward an SUV. "This is me." She fished the keys from her purse, then unlocked the vehicle with the fob. She turned to face him. "You be careful. There's something off about this whole thing. Don't trust anyone."

He smirked at her. "I never do."

Kabul Serena Hotel

Kabul, Afghanistan

Kane lay naked, spreadeagle on his bed at the Kabul Serena Hotel in the Afghan capital. A freshly delivered icepack was serving two purposes now as it lay melting, tucked under his still tender balls. Not only was it continuing its work on the now slight swelling, it was also cooling him, the air conditioning not working as the power had failed. Yet again. Twenty years of fighting and rebuilding, and what little there was to show for it once America and its allies left would be destroyed or in the hands of the enemy within a couple of years if not months.

There was a humming noise and the lights flickered on, the air conditioner roaring to life as if the city were begging to differ with his assessment. He checked his watch. His meeting was in two hours, which gave him plenty of time to get ready and review the files Leroux's team had put together. He hadn't had time to look at them all yet. His itinerary from the moment he left the apartment had been too tight, except for the meeting with his handler. And the more he thought about it, the more he was certain it hadn't been a necessary briefing, but instead was a mother wanting to see her child. Sometimes that was how he felt the relationship was—mother and son, with bullets and bombs.

He rolled out of bed and stepped over to the air conditioner, letting the cool air spill over his naked body, the evaporating sweat rapidly cooling him. He placed a towel on one of the chairs at a corner table then sat, strategically placing the icepack where it would do the most good. He logged into his laptop then scanned his emails, a mix of CIA-generated corporate nonsense that any insurance investigator might expect to receive, along with some spam with embedded links that would take him to different sites on the Internet where he could log in to view covert messages.

He fired back standard replies to the corporate masters at Shaw's of London, the laptop part of the cover. He could hand it over without hesitation if security officials ever demanded he do so, and there would be no evidence he had done anything to hide what he had used it for.

He clicked on one of the spam links that took him to a site guaranteeing to increase his length and girth. He glanced down and shook his head. "That would just make you a bigger target." He scrolled down the page then clicked on Ron Jeremy's face. A login prompt appeared and he entered his user ID and password, then moments later was logged into a secure server.

There was a message from Thorn at the top of the list, sent after he was in the air. He clicked on it and smiled. She was renewing her promise to take his advice and was heading back home. It had him wondering where home was for her. The email also named his buddy Leroux as Control for the mission, which suited him just fine. Not only was Leroux his best friend, which meant he could be trusted to always have his back, Leroux also happened to be the best at what he did, and he thanked God every day that Morrison had pushed his friend into the position of responsibility he now had, recognizing the talent being wasted behind a desk analyzing random reports for patterns. His friend had a brilliant mind, a beautiful mind, and it was finally being used to help his country the way it was meant to.

He pulled up the files Leroux's team had put together, opening the report on the oldest attack. He wasn't concerned with the details—he had already read those. What he *was* concerned with were the new flyovers. He didn't bother watching the footage. That was a waste of time. Instead, he scrolled down to read the analyst's report on what differences they had spotted.

He frowned, nothing of significance noted. He brought up the next report and noted that a new well had been dug and solar panels had been installed, but that had been done by NATO. He cursed. Perhaps his theory was wrong. Perhaps these villagers were indeed innocent. He brought up the file on the third attack and smiled. Unexplained solar panels, rooftop satellite dishes, an above-ground pool, and two new vehicles. An SUV and a box van. He pulled up the images. The SUV was a newer British make, known more for its unreliable sportscars. He chuckled at the stills from the video showing the hood open, repairs evidently already underway.

Serves the bastard right.

It was parked in the courtyard of one of the larger homes, solar panels covering one side of the roof, two different satellite dishes on the other. The analyst noted that significant work had been done to the house, old damage repaired, part of the roof replaced, new windows installed. In fact, where there had been no windows, there now were. Somebody had clearly come into a significant amount of money in the past six weeks. Closeups of the box van could explain why nobody was asking questions. Writing on its side indicated it belonged to the local mosque, a generous donation to silence those who would question the donor's good fortune.

He sent a message to Leroux, requesting another flyover, focusing on the owner of this house, then pulled up the file on the fourth attack. The analyst noted repairs made to at least half the homes in the village, but no ostentatious displays of wealth, no new vehicles, solar panels, or satellite dishes. Kane leaned back, folding his arms and pinching his chin as the software flipped through the pictures showing the repairs. Crumbling walls, damaged roofs, failing retaining walls. All necessary repairs, nothing that would make any one neighbor envious of the other if they already had four sound walls and a watertight roof. He jabbed a finger at the screen. "That's something that village elders do."

He snapped his mouth shut. He had already scanned the room for bugs, but it was always possible he missed something. He brought up the files on the fifth attack, then the sixth, the fifth showing a similar shared improvement, the sixth showing a single benefactor. It had him wondering who would benefit from this week's attack. The entire village, or just one lone soul?

The analyst's summary agreed with his hunch. Payoffs were happening at most of the ambush sites. Leroux had ordered an expanded search beyond the original parameters to see if there were any evidence of this happening before that had gone undetected. Kane wouldn't be surprised if more were found, but it didn't matter. He had enough to go on, and the best place to focus his attention was on the two villages where the wealth wasn't being shared. Stroll into a village where everyone had benefited and begin asking questions would get him nowhere. Go into a village where one person was living a far better life than the rest, some tongues might be willing to wag if enough money were flashed. He sent another message to Leroux, giving his observations, which essentially matched up with the analyst who had prepared the report, along with his intention to visit the two villages in question once his meeting with the Afghan minister was complete.

Kane sent the text message to his translator in the open, all part of a cover for both of them if his phone were examined. It vibrated a moment later.

I'll be in the lobby in 45 minutes.

He sent back a thumbs-up, then launched a routine on the laptop that would clear up anything suspicious should it be examined closely. This wasn't a browser history clean-up. That raised red flags. It was a very selective clean-up that would leave every innocent thing he did intact. He snapped shut the laptop, removed his icepack, and headed for the shower, rehearsing his pitch for why Shaw's of London should be insuring the future infrastructure projects of the fledgling democracy.

Sarwani Residence

Kabul, Afghanistan

Mohammed "Mo" Sarwani hummed happily as he checked himself in the cracked mirror. Their youngest played in the next room, happily giggling at something that made a clanging sound. He was certain she was repeatedly dropping a pot lid. It would have been annoying if anyone else were doing it, but he always delighted in his daughter's laughter.

She was their fourth child, and he and his wife had agreed the last. If Allah blessed them with another, they wouldn't be upset, but they were no longer actively trying. Four was enough. It was a good size to ensure the family's future. With all the violence in his homeland, he fully expected that at least one of them would never see his age. And unfortunately, with the Taliban's resurgence, his two daughters had bleak prospects, which was why he continued to work with the Americans, despite the risk.

It could be their ticket out of this country.

He had high hopes when the Americans and their allies had first arrived, but those were gone. There could be no peace with the Taliban. Any agreements signed with them weren't worth the paper they were written on. The moment the Western troops left, the civil war would erupt anew, and when your enemy was willing to slaughter mercilessly, it was difficult to successfully oppose them when the opposition had morals.

The only way to deal with the Taliban and their kind was to match their level of brutality—massacre every last one of them. Unfortunately, that didn't match up with what their Western allies believed was just. The only hope the country had once NATO left was to embrace the violence and violate the so-called human rights of those who cared not for those same rights. Kill them, torture them if captured, and imprison or kill anyone who cooperated willingly. It was the only hope for peace.

The unfortunate thing was that if they did succeed and remove the Taliban threat, someone would eventually fill the void. Afghanistan's history was one of constant violence. It wasn't a real country. It was merely a landmass with borders drawn by foreigners who couldn't understand the tribal culture that dominated their society. It was a culture that never had democracy, and never wanted it. The Taliban had taken over after the Soviets were forced out by the American supplied and financed Mujahideen, using the very weapons and tactics they had learned fighting the Soviets.

When the Soviets pulled out, leaving a power vacuum that America wasn't willing to fill as their interests were finished, religious fanatics had seized the opportunity. They captured much of the country and showed the world what could happen when true Islamic fundamentalism was allowed to gain power.

If the world had thought Iran was bad, it was nothing compared to what the Taliban had done.

Iran was more of a threat because of the money they had from oil. Fortunately for the world, the only thing Afghanistan had to offer was opium, and a land free of Western influence for groups like Al-Qaeda to train on.

He sat on the edge of the bed, his shoulders slumped. What future was there? They had no natural resources, no factories would ever be built here, and foreign investment would dry up the moment NATO left. He drew a deep breath and held it for a moment. There was no hope for his people, though there might be for his family. If they escaped to America. And it was jobs like he was about to do that would be key.

He forced himself to his feet, checking the mirror one last time. He stepped out of the bedroom and into the living area. The children all jumped to their feet and rushed toward him. He held up a finger. "Wait! Are everyone's hands clean? You don't want to mess up your father's suit now, do you?"

Everyone froze, hands inspected and approved before hugs were exchanged. His wife pointed at the small suitcase near the door.

"Everything's ready. Do you know how long you'll be gone?"

He shook his head. "I never know with these people. It could just be tonight, it could be a couple of days. I have no clue, but I'll have my phone, so I'll let you know as soon as I know."

"Don't forget the party this weekend. You can't miss it."

He glanced over at his eldest son, about to turn thirteen. "I wouldn't dream of it. Don't worry if you don't hear from me, though. There might not be coverage where we're going. If they have a satellite phone, I'll try to get through."

She gave him a hug, holding him a little harder and longer than usual, and he kissed the top of her head.

"Be strong, my love. The more of these jobs I do, the better our chances are of getting out of here."

She eased up on the hug, putting a little space between them, then stared up into his eyes, hers welling with tears. "You keep saying that, yet we're still here."

His chest ached at the vocalizing of his failure. "These things take time. I know it seems I'm making no progress, but every time I'm asked to go out on a job, it means they trust me, and the more they trust me, the more likely it is they'll eventually say yes."

She sighed, her shoulders slumping. "I hope you're right. It's getting more dangerous every day."

"I know." He gave her a peck on the lips. "I have to go now, otherwise I'll be late." He said one final goodbye to the children then grabbed the suitcase and headed out the door, all the more determined to ask the man he had helped on countless occasions whether there was any hope of escaping the hellhole he had been born into.

1st Special Forces Operational Detachment—Delta HQ

Fort Bragg, North Carolina

A.k.a. "The Unit"

Command Sergeant Major Burt "Big Dog" Dawson lay stretched out on the grass, his fiancée, Maggie Harris, beside him, her head laying on his chest. He gently stroked her hair, the tips of his fingers detecting the scar that had held her back for so long. But now she didn't even flinch as he touched it. It had finally become part of her, a part that had been accepted, no longer a constant reminder of how fragile life could be, no longer a trigger taking her back to that day in Paris when she had been shot in the head.

Their wedding plans had been put on hold for so long, he had begun to doubt whether she even wanted to get married anymore, but those concerns had been put to rest recently, and things were back on. He was looking forward to becoming her husband, but part of him was more terrified of the process than any mission he might take part in as the leader of Bravo Team, part of 1st Special Forces Operational Detachment—Delta, more commonly known to the public as Delta Force.

An engine roared behind them but he didn't bother looking. He recognized it as Sergeant Will "Spock" Lightman's 1972 'Cuda in original Barracuda Orange. It was his pride and joy, recently acquired, the day he had purchased it one filled with precious memories of when he rode as a child with his father in the same make, model, and year. He only took it out on days when the weather would be perfect, like today. Blue skies, only a few wisps of clouds with a gentle breeze, an idyllic day for a barbecue behind the Unit.

He and Maggie had arrived half an hour early so that he could get the oil drum barbecues going, then enjoy a little bit of alone time, the apartment they lived in lacking a yard, the sliver of a balcony providing little enjoyment of the outdoors.

"Fun's over."

Maggie patted his chest. "Or has it just begun?"

He shrugged. "I suppose there are two ways to look at everything."

She rolled off him and stood, waving at Spock and his wife, Joanne. "Hi, guys!"

"Hi, Maggie! Hi, BD!" replied Joanne, Spock offering a wave and a smile.

Dawson rose. Hugs and handshakes exchanged as he admired the pristine Barracuda, parked beside his own 1964½ Mustang convertible in original poppy red, his own pride and joy inherited from his father in equally pristine condition.

Everyone turned as another vehicle arrived with Sergeant Leon "Atlas" James and his girlfriend, Vanessa Moore, behind the wheel of her purple Nissan Micra, about to provide a hilarious moment as it pulled in beside the other cars. Vanessa climbed out of the driver's seat and beamed a smile at the others as the massively muscled Atlas threw open the passenger side door and stared at them helplessly.

Dawson eyed him. "I've got two questions."

"They'd better be good," rumbled Atlas in his impossibly deep voice.

"Where's your car?"

"In the shop. And your other question?"

"Just how in the hell did you get in there in the first place?"

Atlas frowned. "Believe it or not, getting in was relatively easy."

Vanessa batted a hand at him as Sergeant Eugene "Jagger" Thomas pulled up. "Oh, quit complaining. You're telling me a super-soldier can't get out of a tight situation?"

Dawson extended a hand and Atlas waved it off. "No, the car's in the shop for at least a few days. I need to figure this out."

Jagger walked over and leaned in, examining his friend's predicament. "Too bad Niner isn't here. We could use him as a shoehorn."

Dawson chuckled and Atlas growled. "You're not helping." He grabbed his right leg and struggled to lift it out to no avail. He was wedged in good. "I think my legs are asleep." He sighed. "To hell with it." He leaned hard to his right, twisting his entire body before dropping his hands onto the pavement then hand-walking his way out, dragging the rest of his body along with him. He flipped over onto his back, staring up at his two comrades-in-arms. "Are you two just going to stand there, or are you going to help a brother up?"

Dawson and Jagger extended hands, then pulled their friend to his feet. Atlas took a couple of tentative steps, letting the circulation return as Dawson stared into the interior of the ridiculously tiny car. It reminded him of his youth. His parents had bought a second car, a Renault R5, a tiny little French thing that they said he could drive. He had been horrified at the idea, but the next day at school, he had walked through the parking lot and saw some of the cars the other kids were driving, and he didn't feel as bad about it.

And the freedom it would give him was worth the possible embarrassment. So, the next day he had driven it to school, parked it, and went inside. Nobody said anything. Nobody made fun of him, despite the ridiculously tiny car having a decal across the bottom of the doors reading "Le Car," just in case anyone confused it with a riding lawnmower.

And he drove a girl home, confirming the benefits of having wheels no matter how they looked.

What was hilarious was that the next day, when he came to school and parked, he found four other Renault Le Cars scattered through the parking lot. No one had had the balls to drive theirs to school until someone else did. He had never felt self-conscious about the car from then on.

But he wasn't a muscled monster like his friend Atlas. Cars like that were never designed for men like him.

More arrived, families unloading, the green space behind the Unit quickly filling with the laughter of children as the men, their partners, their families, gathered, providing a perfect example of what they put their lives on the line for every day.

This was America.

Families made up of all races, creeds, and colors, doing whatever it took to fight against those who would take it away. He loved his country and would die for it, as would any of the men here. Was it perfect? By no means, yet was any country perfect? People were too entrenched in their positions these days, and after hearing Professor James Acton rant about social media, Dawson was convinced it was the problem as well.

Everything was filtered. Most people had no clue that what they saw on their social media feeds was based on algorithms designed to show them things the computer thought were of interest to them or would make them happy. It detected that they always clicked Like on an article blaming mankind for climate change for example, or instead on an article questioning man's involvement. The algorithm quickly learned this, then only showed them articles that they were most likely to approve of. It meant that those who liked the articles blaming man for climate change only ever saw stories or postings from friends who favored that position and never saw anything challenging it. And the reverse was true as well.

What it meant was, when someone heard an opposing opinion, they assumed that person was an idiot because every single story they had ever seen supported their side. Yet that wasn't the reality. There were a mix of views on every subject, and they weren't just "yes" or "no." There were various shades of "maybe" out there. But in a society where everything was yes or no, like or dislike, thumbs up or thumbs down, it led to thinking in similar terms. Right or wrong, black or white, good or evil. And everybody always thought they were on the side of good, which meant that those that disagreed with them or opposed them were clearly evil, and evil must be destroyed in all its forms.

Yet that wasn't life. That wasn't reality.

And until people learned that fact, that there were algorithms designed by social media companies intent on making people happy so they would stay on the platform so they could earn more advertising revenue, he feared his country was doomed to be torn apart.

As he stared at the growing crowd, however, it gave him hope. This was what America could be if it remembered the way things used to be. Again, not perfect, but at least with civil discourse. When neighbors who have lived beside each other for decades now hate each other because of the lawn sign they put out every four years, there was a problem. When families could no longer attend holiday dinners together because of who they voted for, there was a problem.

A throaty engine roared, interrupting his thoughts, and he turned to see Sergeant Carl "Niner" Sung pulling in with his new girlfriend, Angela Henwood, in a massive Ford F-250.

"I think someone's over-compensating," grumbled Atlas.

Snickers rippled through the group as Niner hopped out and Angela climbed down. Master Sergeant Mike "Red" Belme walked up with his wife and son, admiring Niner's new truck.

"What does over-compensating mean?" asked young Bryson Belme.

More snickers.

Atlas was about to say something that would no doubt be inappropriate, but Dawson raised a hand, cutting him off as he noticed Niner's somber expression and Angela's red eyes. The others spotted it as well, and the adults quickly quietened, the parents sending any children nearby onto the ball diamond.

"What's wrong?" asked Dawson.

Niner frowned. "You heard about that ambush in Afghanistan a couple of days ago?"

Everyone nodded.

"I just heard Dax was one of them."

There were several gasps. A few of the spouses who had been attached to the Unit for a while cried out and the children fell silent without knowing why. Dax Laurier had been a good friend, a member of Charlie Team. He had joined Delta around the same time Dawson had. With the birth of his second child, his wife had begged him to leave the Unit. It was too dangerous. He had reluctantly agreed, though on condition he could still serve in the Army, and the man most of them knew well had returned to the regular forces where he was supposed to be safer.

Tears flowed down Maggie's cheeks. In her position as Colonel Clancy's assistant, she had met Dax on many occasions. "His poor family!"

Spock sighed heavily. "Well, this kind of puts a damper on things."

"Maybe we should pack it up and do this another day," suggested his wife.

Dawson held up a hand, everyone falling silent. "We lost a good man, and we lost five other good men and women in that same attack, but that's the job. And no one knew that more than Dax, who died doing what he loved. Now, for those of you who never met him, he was a great guy. He loved his wife and children, loved the Unit, loved his country." He jabbed a finger toward the barbecues. "And the man loved his barbecue."

Chuckles rippled through the group.

"I miss his ribs," said Atlas. He turned to his girlfriend, Vanessa, training to be a chef. "He had this homemade sauce that was unbelievable. You would have loved it."

She beamed up at him, her eyes glistening as she patted his chest. "I'm sure I would have."

"So, here's what I propose," said Dawson. "We don't mourn the man. We celebrate the man. We were planning on burgers and dogs. I say we go pick up some ribs and do this thing right."

Some whoops and cheers were followed by clapping as everyone psyched themselves up for what was to come, a brave face, forced for now, that would turn into a mix of laughter and tears as they reminisced over the coming hours about their friend.

I'll miss you, Dax.

Ministry of Urban Development and Land
3rd Macrorayon, Kabul, Afghanistan

Kane stepped outside, staring down at the courtyard in front of the Soviet-era office building where the Minister of Urban Development and Land held court. He glanced over at the translator he had worked with for years, Mo. "Well, there's an hour we'll never get back."

Mo chuckled. "I think you had him almost convinced that Shaw's was indeed willing to underwrite their new construction projects, despite the fact the Taliban had vowed to blow every one of them up."

Kane headed down the steps. "Yeah, sometimes I forget what my job is."

"Where to now?"

"The Wakhan Corridor."

Mo's eyes widened. "The Wakhan Corridor? Where those soldiers were ambushed a few days ago?"

"Yeah."

"Doesn't that mean the area's not safe?"

Kane shook his head. "Oddly enough, I don't think it does, unless you're wearing an American uniform and going to a scheduled meeting."

Mo stared at him, puzzled. "When my wife is viewing my body, she might appreciate a clearer explanation than that."

Kane slapped him on the back, grinning. "Where's that positive attitude you're famous for?"

Mo grunted. "Oh, it's still there. I'm positive that one of these days you're going to get me killed."

Kane climbed in the armored SUV his cover company had arranged for him. It was a beast on gas, but it would protect them from small arms fire. He started the engine as Mo closed the passenger door and put his seatbelt on. Kane turned to him, serious. "Listen, if you're having second thoughts, I can find someone else."

Mo rapidly shook his head. "No, please don't. I need this job. It feeds my family, and…" He hesitated.

"And you hope it'll get you out of the country?"

Mo stared at the dash. "Will it?"

Kane put the vehicle in gear and pulled away. "The paperwork's been submitted, and I've asked my contacts to see if they can goose the process along. Beyond that, there's not much more I can do."

Mo sighed. "Things are getting worse here, not better. I'm terrified that once you guys leave, the government will fall, and the people like me who cooperated will be hunted down then tortured and killed along with our families."

Kane came to a halt behind another car waiting near the gate and regarded the man he had been on missions with at least a dozen times. Rarely were they under fire, though there had been enough hairy situations that Mo had plenty of opportunity to prove his courage and his trustworthiness. So many of the translators here had pledged their loyalty to the new government and its foreign allies, with the expectation that the government would never fall because of its NATO backing. And many, like Mo, were being abandoned as the troop drawdown continued.

Yet what choice did America and its allies have? It had been two decades. It was ridiculous. If a country couldn't be stabilized in that amount of time, it was clear the population didn't want it, and if that were the case, then so be it. But they shouldn't be abandoning those who had helped them, those they knew would be targets.

But these things were beyond his control. That was for politicians to decide. He didn't make policy, he enforced it, though perhaps there were favors he could call in that he hadn't yet. He reached over and grabbed Mo by the shoulder, giving it a squeeze and a shake. "Have faith, my friend. Let's get through the next week or so, and then I'll make some more phone calls."

Mo's reaction wasn't what he had expected. Instead of a smile or a thank you, his eyes bugged out. "A *week* or so?"

Kane nodded as he pulled through the gates and onto the road, heading back toward his hotel. "It could be a little bit longer, but I have a feeling I'm going to have the answers I need within a week."

Mo muttered a prayer to Allah, pleading for strength as he dialed his cellphone.

"Something wrong?" asked Kane.

"I have to tell my wife how long I'm going to be away. I assured her it wouldn't be more than a few days. She's going to be most upset."

Kane laughed. "Buddy, we've been gone for weeks before."

"Yes, but that's before we had our fourth child. I promised her I wouldn't do that again. And it's my eldest's thirteenth birthday."

Kane's chest tightened as he offered his congratulations for the milestone, yet another reason he had to get this family out of a country that would see its men slaughtered for doing the right thing, and deny its women any semblance of human rights should those trapped a thousand years in the past retake control.

Baharak Bazaar

Baharak, Afghanistan

Jafar sat, struggling to control his nerves. The attack hadn't gone as planned. Their village's imam was dead. Half a dozen of those involved in the attack were also, and several of the elders had been wounded when those who claimed to be their friends opened fire indiscriminately on the imam's home.

It had been a bloodbath.

None of that would have happened if the ambush had taken place outside of their community as had been planned. He didn't care that the Americans had been betrayed. Despite being on friendly terms with them for years, they were an occupying force, and now they were leaving. His village had to make plans for the future, a future where the Taliban would be in control, and the only way to survive under their dominion was to keep your head down and obey their rules.

So, when in Baharak, negotiating for supplies with some of the money the American soldiers had left them with a few weeks ago, he had lent his ear when approached by the man now scrolling through the photos. The proposal had been simple. Let him know when the next scheduled meeting was, and provide a dozen able-bodied men to participate in the attack with a small contingent that would arrive the morning of the ambush.

And for every American killed, he would pay an unfathomable amount of money. Typically, six Americans would come for the meetings. It would mean so much for his village. And it would be for his village, for he had no intention of keeping the money himself. It was a cruel, evil act they would be participating in, betraying those who came to them in friendship, and executing them for profit. Though if the money were used for the village, then perhaps it could be justified. After all, their late imam had taught that only believers were worthy, and if betrayal of one's word were necessary, it was only permitted if a non-believer were involved.

Yet it wasn't a decision he could make. He wasn't an elder. The man had given him a phone and a number with instructions to call him as soon as a decision had been made. He had finished purchasing the supplies and returned to his village. When he arrived, he had immediately sought out the imam and the village elders. He told them what had been said, and a raging debate ensued that went well into the night.

But a decision had finally been made. NATO was pulling out, which meant they had no defense against the Taliban or anyone else should someone take an interest in the village. New allegiances were needed. If they refused these people, they could become targets, but if they agreed, they would be richly awarded, hopefully protected after the Americans pulled out, and the only cost would be the lives of a few infidels who had no business being in Afghanistan.

They agreed the money would be used to improve the lives of everyone in the village, especially the families of those who might be martyred in the ambush. Jafar had immediately agreed to be among the volunteers demanded of the man, though he had been refused. He was the point of contact. It was essential he stay alive, take the photos demanded, and get them to their contact. Involving anyone else risked linking the village to what would be an atrocity in the eyes of the Americans they were betraying.

And it had been an atrocity.

The Americans had figured out something was wrong, attempted to pull out early, and died regardless. But so had the imam he had known his entire life. From his refuge in the hills, he had watched on in horror as those who had been sent in to join them, who had provided the weapons and trained them, opened fire on the imam's home indiscriminately.

The entire event hadn't taken ten minutes. The moment the last shot had been fired, he rushed down from his perch, took his photos, then fled with the rest of the village before the Americans arrived. He had come into the city the next day, made his phone call, and was now sitting in the mosque's supply truck, his heart hammering as each photo was examined.

The man smiled as he turned to face him. "Excellent work. Six as you said on the phone." He gestured toward the bag clutched against Jafar's chest. "You've got your money. We agreed I'd pay you one thousand per American, so that's six thousand to you in there. A profitable day for a few minutes work."

Jafar nodded.

"You have our thanks, and a promise that we won't interfere in the affairs of your village, as long as you don't defy us."

Jafar gulped. "Who is us?"

The man chuckled. "You don't need to know." He tapped the bag. "You're sure you don't want to count it?"

Jafar gulped again. He could try, but he wasn't sure he could count high enough for it to matter. "No, I trust you."

The man smiled broadly, slapping him on the back. "Excellent. Now, I'm sure I don't need to tell you this, but we never met, you were never paid, you never participated in the attack. You're victims, just like the Americans."

Jafar opened his mouth to pose an obvious question, then decided against it.

"You were about to ask me something. We're all friends here. Ask your question."

Jafar patted his bag. "How do we explain this?"

"Don't be stupid, and you won't have to. Wait a while, then use it wisely."

"But what if we're asked? This is more money than our village has ever seen in its entire history."

64

"Then tell them you found it."

Jafar stared at him for a moment. "Where would I find something like this?"

"There was a government convoy hit last week in your region. Just tell them you came upon it, found the money, and decided to donate it to your mosque. No one would dare challenge you on it. Any more questions?"

Jafar shook his head.

"Good. You'll never see me again unless you betray me, and then I'll be the last thing you ever see." The man climbed out then slammed the door shut, disappearing among the crowds.

Jafar peered into the bag then grabbed the thick envelope sitting on top, opening it once again, his pulse racing at the amount it contained. He stuffed it into an inner pocket and prayed he wasn't searched on the way home. He started the engine then put the old beast in gear, and as he pulled away, the transmission grinding with each shift, he hoped the village elders decided some of the money should be invested into a new vehicle. As he gained speed, heading out of the city and onto the lonely road that led to the village he called home, the thought of a new vehicle brought a smile, the future comfort eagerly looked forward to.

And all that it cost were the lives of six infidels and one traitor to his country.

The Unit

Fort Bragg, North Carolina

"Go on in, he's expecting you."

Command Sergeant Major Dawson winked at his fiancée Maggie as she waved him into his commanding officer's inner sanctum. He rapped twice on the closed door, his hand perched over the knob.

"Enter!"

He dropped his hand and turned the knob, pushing the door aside. Colonel Thomas Clancy glanced up from his computer then directed him with a finger into one of the chairs in front of his desk. Dawson closed the door and took a seat as Clancy finished reading something before turning his attention to Dawson.

"Sergeant Major, you asked to see me?"

"Yes, sir. It's about Dax."

Clancy leaned back, frowning. "So, you've heard."

"Yes, sir. I suspect the entire base has heard by now."

"I suppose they have. And before you ask, at the moment, we have no idea who committed the attack, so we don't know if it was Taliban." Clancy tapped a finger on his desk for a moment, contemplating something, then leaned forward, lowering his voice. "I'm going to tell you something off the record. Don't repeat this to anybody, including Maggie."

Dawson pulled his chair closer. "My lips are sealed."

"The captain in charge of the mission managed to communicate that he thought the villagers were in on it. We have drone footage from after the attack showing someone taking photos of the bodies of our people."

Dawson's eyebrows shot up. "Photos? Like recruitment photos?"

Clancy shrugged. "We don't know, but this wasn't the first time this has happened in the past couple of months. Langley's investigating, as is the Pentagon. Something strange is going on, and we need to find out what, because our people are being targeted in areas that have been peaceful for far too long." He leaned back and folded his arms. "So, just why are you here, Sergeant Major?"

Dawson sat upright. "Bravo Team is requesting that if there's a mission, we're part of it."

Clancy regarded him. "Don't you think Charlie Team should have that honor?"

"Absolutely, but if it takes more than them, Bravo Team would like the honor of accompanying them."

Clancy smiled at him. "I wouldn't have it any other way."

Wakhan Corridor, Afghanistan

Kane shifted in the driver's seat, grunting, the boys still a little tender, though now it was only if he worked them into an odd position or bounced them around too much. And this poor excuse for a road was doing a Tommy Lee drum solo on them.

"Are you all right?" asked Mo. "If I didn't know any better, I'd say you were in pain."

Kane shifted again. "My girlfriend shot me in the nuts a couple of days ago."

Mo's eyes bulged. "What?"

Kane roared with laughter. "Paintball, not real bullets."

"What's paintball?"

"It's a game where you run around and pretend to be soldiers and shoot at each other with little balls of paint."

Mo shook his head. "You Americans are so strange. Why would anybody want to make a game out of something as horrible as war?"

Kane regarded the man for a moment. It was an interesting question. He could honestly say he had no clue whether something like paintball was popular outside of America, or whether young people glued to their video game consoles, simulating war, was exclusive to children raised in peaceful countries where they had no concept of what war was. He shrugged. "I don't know. I suppose when you're surrounded by war every day, it's inconceivable to think anyone would want to simulate it for fun."

Mo gestured toward Kane's genitals. "For your girlfriend to have shot you there, you must have really upset her."

Kane chuckled. "I had just shot her in the tatas, and in her defense, she thought I was wearing a cup."

Mo eyed him. "Why would one wear a cup over one's private parts?"

Kane roared again. "Different kind of cup, my friend."

Mo shook his head. "If I ever get to America, I fear it's going to be a difficult place to understand."

"Yes, but you'll be safe. Your wife and daughters will be safe, and they'll have futures that won't be limited simply because they're women."

Mo pressed his head against the back of his seat and sighed. "I can't imagine it. Every time I hear an American or someone from one of the Western countries talking, it seems like a dream, like propaganda designed to make the rest of the world believe your way of life is better than it actually is, just so they can prove they're on the right side of whatever conflict they're in."

Kane grunted. "Well, we're certainly not perfect by any stretch of the imagination, but we're a hell of a lot better than most of the world. Unfortunately, we've become polarized to the extreme, and it's ruining things. It's a crying shame, really, and I pray every day we come to our senses before it's too late."

"Polarized? How so?"

"An old professor of mine blames social media, and says America is particularly susceptible to the binary culture being created by it through everything only having two options. Yes or no, like or dislike, thumbs up or thumbs down. It conditions our way of thinking into believing there are only two choices in life."

Mo regarded him. "So, if I'm right and your opinion is different, then you must be wrong?"

"Exactly. And it goes beyond that. Too many think they're on the side of good, therefore you must be evil if you disagree. And it extends into politics. Most stable democracies have several reasonable choices on the ballot. For generations, America has only had two, and it fits into this binary way of thinking. If I support one party and you support the other, then you must be either evil, stupid, or uninformed. There can't be any in-between. It's tearing apart what's supposed to be the greatest nation on Earth."

Mo frowned. "Why is this the first I'm hearing of it?"

"It's not exactly something we're proud of, but the problems in Western society aren't exclusive to America, though we seem to be taking the brunt of it at the moment. Unfortunately, anyone who speaks out to challenge any of the extreme viewpoints on both sides is canceled."

Mo eyed him. "Canceled?"

"They're attacked on social media and their careers are destroyed. The problem is that it doesn't take many to destroy a career. Get a few hundred people in an outrage over nothing who have followers, and they pile on. It causes something to trend, and before you know it, you have millions of people demanding someone lose their job, yet they don't even know why they're demanding it, because they never bother researching the issue or even reading the article. They're simply agreeing because some Hollywood simpleton says they should be angry. Like my father always said, just because you have a following doesn't mean you're smart."

"In Afghanistan, we don't really have anything like that, though I suppose our politicians have followings, and I can say with certainty the majority of them have no brains."

Kane chuckled. "That, my friend, is something shared the world over."

The GPS interrupted their conversation, giving its first direction in at least an hour. Their destination was just ahead. Kane geared down and pulled them over to the side of the poor excuse for a road, riddled with potholes and temporary repairs. It gave him an idea for his cover story. He grabbed a set of binoculars then climbed out. "You stay here. I'm only going to be a couple of minutes. Honk the horn if anything happens. There's a gun in the center console. It's a Glock, so don't go looking for the safety, just aim and shoot."

Mo's face slackened slightly, but he nodded. Kane closed the door then scurried up a rise on the opposite side of the road, gaining the high ground for a better perspective. He crawled the last few yards then lay prone on the uncomfortable rock-strewn ground. He peered at the village ahead, doing a quick scan for anything that could prove dangerous, then did a slow pass, picking out the landmarks from the reports he had read, the hillside from where the attack had initiated, the village center scarred by the Humvee explosion, and the building where Dax and his captain had been killed, still pockmarked with bullet holes.

He didn't spot any red flags. Nobody was walking around with guns or acting suspiciously. It appeared to be an ordinary, peaceful Afghan village, desperately impoverished with people who just wanted to be left alone.

Gears ground behind him and he rolled to his side, redirecting his binoculars. An old transport truck with a threadbare canvas back was slowing as it approached his SUV. He rose and slung the binoculars over his shoulder and behind his back as he rushed down the hillside. The truck came to a stop and a man about his age climbed out, not yet noticing him, approaching the driver's side window. Pleasantries were exchanged in Pashto, the man introducing himself as Jafar and asking Mo if everything were all right.

"Hello," called Kane, raising his hand with a practiced smile that won most people over. The man spun, fear written on his face. Kane raised his hands slightly, showing them empty. "Mo, let him know I'm friendly," he said in English, despite speaking Pashto—his cover didn't.

"He's an American civilian. He's a friend," said Mo, who then made proper introductions.

Jafar relaxed slightly. He jerked his chin toward where Kane had just come from, asking what he had been doing. Kane waited for the translation. "I was just relieving myself." He swung the binoculars around. "And I was checking your road. It's not in good shape, is it?"

Jafar shook his head. "It never has been for as long as I've been alive." He eyed him. "Are you here to repair the road?"

Kane shook his head and Jafar was clearly disappointed. Kane smiled. "I'm here to *replace* the road."

Jafar's face brightened as Mo translated. "Then I must take you to the elders! Follow me and I'll introduce you. It will be better that way."

Kane agreed, and a two-vehicle convoy was quickly formed. They were inside the village within minutes, his expert eye surveying everything close-up as pleasantries were exchanged. They were invited into the very home where Dax had made his last stand and lost. Kane had met Dax on many occasions during his brief stint in Delta before being recruited into the CIA. Dax was a good man, a family man, and reading that he was one of the victims had been a gut punch.

He kept his practiced smile in place as he was introduced to those perhaps responsible for the deaths of six Americans and their translator only days before. Jafar turned to a young man, telling him the supplies to repair the walls were in the truck, and the man rushed outside. Kane and Mo, along with several of the elders, sat on carpets laid out on the dirt floor, and he suppressed a frown at a dark stain on the trim of one of them that appeared to be blood.

Whose blood was it? Dax's? Captain O'Donnell's? Or one of those that had lured them into the trap? A space directly across from him in the circle being formed remained empty, and Kane surreptitiously surveyed the room, spotting out of the corner of his eye Jafar handing over a thick envelope to an elderly man who tucked it into his robes with a smile before taking the empty spot.

"This is our new imam," explained Jafar. "I'll take my leave of you now."

Kane thanked him and Jafar headed outside. He returned his attention to those seated with them, smiling pleasantly as his well-trained eyes assessed the body language on display. There was a certain uneasiness in the room. Excitement was evident, which could sometimes be mistaken for nervousness. They had, after all, just been told they might be getting a freshly paved road into their village.

But it was more than that, at least with the imam, whose eyes were wide, the smile on his face far too genuine. He was excited about something, and it had to be the thick envelope he had been handed, an envelope that suspiciously resembled a wrapped stack of bills. Kane was certain the man had just been delivered a payoff, though there was no way he could prove that, nor could he challenge the man. All he could do was keep up the pretense of being here to discuss the new road, for if it were indeed a payoff, it proved these people couldn't be trusted, and wouldn't hesitate to kill to keep their secret.

Jafar grabbed the last of the supplies from the back of the truck, handing it over to one of the others. It was the most expensive load of supplies he had ever returned with, some of the payoff used to purchase materials to repair the roofs on all the houses. He couldn't wait. The house he shared with four generations of his family was in desperate need. There were far too many holes in their roof, patched over the years. Heat would escape at night in the summer or all day in the winter, animals would get in, and rain was a constant problem.

As it was for everyone.

They were all poor farmers, eking out a meager living by bartering for what they needed with any surplus crops. The money received earlier today would do so much good, improving the lives of all. He glanced over at the home of his best friend, Behrooz, that sat near the center of the village, scarred by bullets and flame from when the rocket had hit the Americans' vehicle. The supplies he had purchased included what would be needed to erase any evidence of what had happened here earlier in the week, and soon they would put this entire affair behind them.

He placed his hands on his hips and stretched his back, thrusting his pelvis forward. His gaze came to rest on the SUV that had brought the American and his translator. He couldn't believe their good fortune. He was pretty sure he was 30 years old, though there was some dispute over that. His mother said 30, his father said 31. Whatever it was, the road had been the road for as long as he had been alive. When the Americans had arrived years ago, repairs had been made, though he was convinced it wasn't for the benefit of the locals, but for their own vehicles to have a smoother ride.

He continued to stare at the vehicle, the one lone vehicle with no government markings, the single vehicle with nothing that indicated its purpose, carrying two unarmed men. This region was normally peaceful. The only violence he had heard about in years was the attack he had participated in several days ago. Surely these people were aware of the incident, but if they were, why would they come here with no guards, no security, no defense, especially here specifically, where the attack had occurred? Could they be that ignorant? If they knew the truth, then they would know there was no real risk. If they knew the truth, then they would know there was little danger. However, there was no way they could know the truth, yet here they were.

Was it possible they didn't know about what had happened? Even if so, he couldn't recall the last time he had seen any foreigner alone, unarmed. He pursed his lips as he scratched at his beard. It made no sense. It was one thing to be brave, though too often foolishness was mistaken for courage. The man could be new to the country and ignorant to the dangers, though he had to work for people who had experience, who wouldn't send their new worker into a dangerous situation.

None of it made sense.

His head swiveled, checking for anyone watching, then he strode as casually as he could manage toward the SUV. It appeared locked though he didn't dare touch it. He had, of course, heard of car alarms, though the few vehicles in the village weren't equipped. Instead, he peered through the windows, searching for anything out of place, but it was what he didn't find that had his suspicions growing. Where was the paperwork? Government people always had paperwork. Forms, pamphlets, booklets, badges, identification, and so much more, yet there wasn't anything, not a single piece in sight, and there were no briefcases or file holders where they might be hiding.

Yet still, he couldn't be certain that was anything suspicious. He had never worked for the government, and his interactions in this area were mainly with the American military, who did not understand that when they handed out pamphlets, there was almost nobody in the village who could actually read them. Perhaps these new arrivals weren't so ignorant.

A foot scraped behind him on the gravel and his heart leaped into his throat as he spun. He breathed a sigh of relief to find it was his friend Behrooz.

"What are you doing?"

Jafar shook his head. "Nothing. Just curious."

Behrooz cupped his hands against the glass and peered inside.

Jafar gasped. "Careful, you might set the alarm off!"

Behrooz shrugged. "So? If they're supposed to be our friends, aren't we allowed to be curious?"

Jafar eyed him. "If?"

Behrooz gave him a look. "Don't play stupid with me. I've known you your entire life. You think there's something wrong, otherwise why would you be staring so intently inside this car and perhaps risking a new road?"

Jafar said nothing.

Behrooz smirked. "Your silence speaks volumes, my friend." He pointed at the road running through their village. "You and I both know nobody's going to be building us a new road when there are so many others that are far more important that need to be done."

Jafar's head bobbed slowly as he thought about it. It didn't make sense. Their road was terrible, yes, but the road led to scattered villages of no importance and a closed Chinese border. There were entire highways in the region in need of replacement where transport trucks and other vehicles traveled regularly. He paused. Why had the man been up on the hill with binoculars? He said he had been surveying the road, yet he had just driven on it.

The more he thought about it, the more nothing made sense. American soldiers die in his village, and several days later, a lone American civilian and his Afghan translator show up alone and unarmed, claiming to be doing work on replacing a road that no one had cared about for decades. Every government official he had ever met, every Westerner he had ever met, always had a badge or a uniform. They always presented it when they arrived, but that hadn't happened here.

Jafar shook his head. "You're right. Something's wrong here."

Behrooz pointed up. "There's another thing that's wrong."

Jafar tilted his head back and peered up at the sky. "What?"

Behrooz pointed and Jafar squinted, finally spotting what his friend already had—a drone circling overhead. "Now, tell me, is that there because of them, or is that there because of what we did to those Americans?"

The blood drained from Jafar's cheeks as his jaw dropped. "Or are they both here because of what we did to those Americans?"

Operations Center 2, CIA Headquarters

Langley, Virginia

"I think they made us."

Leroux cursed at Child's observation. Two men that had been paying a little bit too much attention to Kane's SUV were now staring directly at the drone overhead. He reached for his headset to warn Kane and cursed again. He wasn't on comms. But there was a relay in his SUV that could communicate with his watch. He turned to Tong. "Send him an emergency signal indicating he might have been made."

Tong typed furiously on her keyboard for a few moments then gave a thumbs-up. "Message sent."

Leroux stared at the screen. The two men were still peering up at the drone, and he debated what he should do. He could call it off, which might appear suspicious, or he could leave it in place, which could stoke the villagers' suspicions regardless.

He had to leave it in place. He had to know what was going on. It was the only way they could send in help should Kane need it. He glanced at Tong. "Any acknowledgment?"

She shook her head. "No, though if he's in a room full of people, I wouldn't expect any."

Leroux stared back at the screen, several more villagers joining the other two men, all staring up at the drone.

This can't be good.

Wakhan Corridor, Afghanistan

The brief discussion held so far had been polite, the village elders and their imam clearly excited with the prospect of a new road. Yet it was evident to Kane something more was going on here. The imam continued his unconscious touching of the envelope, suspiciously shaped like a stack of bills, and too many people were avoiding eye contact, as if they had something to feel guilty or ashamed about.

It was everything he could do not to stare at the bloodstain on the carpet he sat on, the question of whose blood it was gnawing at him. Was it his friend Dax's, Captain O'Donnell's, the dead imam's, or someone else's entirely? Yet blood on a carpet wasn't proof of complicity or active involvement.

But what was in that envelope could be.

He listened as Mo translated for the elders, their biggest concern the confirmation of a timeline and that it would cost them nothing. Kane's watch sent a gentle electrical pulse into his wrist, but this time it was in a coded pattern that he rarely received, indicating his mission might be compromised. He waited for Mo to finish the translation, then stood. "I'll find out the dates for you. I just need to use the satellite phone in our vehicle to make a call."

Mo moved to stand but Kane waved him off. If the mission were compromised, he needed to get to his weapon before he could help either of them. Raising suspicions at this point wouldn't help anyone. He held out his hand, indicating for Mo to remain behind, but showed him two fingers. Mo's eyes picked up on the prearranged signal they had used for years, his eyes flaring slightly. He explained to the elders what was happening as Kane ignored the conversation he wasn't supposed to understand.

He wasn't overly concerned with the elders. If the mission were compromised, it wasn't from inside that room. Something had to have happened outside. He pushed aside the carpet doubling as a door and stepped out into the bright sunlight to discover a dozen villagers staring up at the sky, too many of them standing beside his SUV. He crossed the village center unnoticed, all eyes on the drone feeding Langley.

Jafar noticed him first. He stabbed a finger toward the drone circling overhead. "Why is that here? Are you American spies?" he shouted in Pashto.

Kane feigned ignorance, though the pointed finger demanded to be acknowledged. He continued toward the SUV, the fob in his hand, and glanced up at the sky and waved two fingers in the air, something those back in Langley should pick up on.

"Don't worry about him, gentlemen, he's just here to make sure nothing happens to me." One in the crowd spoke English and translated, the tension easing. "I just need to make a phone call to find out when we can put your road in." Kane unlocked the doors, the lights flashing, and he climbed inside, closing the door behind him. He leaned over and opened the glove compartment, pulling out a satellite phone and holding it up for the curious onlookers. He dialed, and moments later the call was answered.

"Shaw's of London, how may I direct your call?"

"Extension four-seven-two-six, please."

"And who may I say is calling?"

"Dylan Kane." The use of his real name indicated the line wasn't secure at his end. Somebody on the other side of the reinforced glass might hear him or might read lips. The only thing he could be sure of was that they wouldn't hear the other side of the conversation. The call was put through and answered immediately.

"Hello?"

He recognized Leroux's voice. "Hey, buddy, it's me. Just calling in to see if you had those estimates on when the road would make it to this area."

"I take it you got my signal?"

"Yes, I did."

"We noticed some villagers trying to look inside your vehicle then getting a little anxious over the UAV. We recommend you leave immediately."

"We should be able to do that," replied Kane. "Hopefully in about sixty days."

"Sixty seconds, understood." Leroux cursed. "Check your six."

Kane glanced in the rearview mirror and spotted a man emerging from a nearby house, an AK-47 gripped in his hand. He aimed it at the sky and opened fire. Kane glanced at those surrounding him, everyone's attention no longer directed at him. He opened the center console and pulled out his Glock and three extra mags. He stuffed the weapon in his belt behind his back and the mags in his left pocket. He turned toward the home where the meeting was being held, certain his mental count was already at two minutes.

Come on, Mo, where the hell are you?

Mo sat cross-legged on the carpet, smiling uncomfortably as the half-dozen men in the room stared at him, the friendly smiles on display for the American gone. Even if these men didn't support the Taliban, few Afghans supported foreigners on their soil.

To them, he was a traitor.

He counted down in his head, perhaps a little too slowly, though he couldn't risk checking his watch. He was approaching ten seconds left when gunfire erupted outside. He scrambled to his feet, everyone in the room appearing equally as shocked as him, which suggested this wasn't an ambush like earlier in the week.

"I'll go see what's happening," he said, rushing toward the door before anyone had a chance to protest. He emerged into the sunlight, squinting. There were at least a dozen people on the street, one man firing an AK-47 in the air, appearing to be aiming carefully as opposed to firing in celebration of something. Kane was nowhere to be seen, and the reflection off the windshield prevented him from confirming he was inside their SUV. He strode swiftly toward the passenger side of the vehicle, not bothering to look up at what was likely the UAV tasked to monitor them, and passed several of the locals before someone finally noticed.

"Hey, where are you going?"

He kept moving forward, calmly, careful not to pick up his pace. He smiled at the man challenging him. "Just making sure my friend's all right. Gunfire makes him nervous."

More were now paying attention to him. "Maybe you should ask him why the Americans are spying on us."

Mo continued forward, though was forced to slow his pace as someone approached him. He side-stepped them but was blocked by another. He came to a halt and looked up at the sky, spotting the UAV. "Is that what you're concerned about?"

Jafar threw his hands up in the air. "Of course we're concerned about it! You claim to be here on behalf of the government, yet you spy on us?"

Mo's heart was pounding now, but so far, no one had been truly threatening, and only one gun was in sight, and it was still belching lead uselessly skyward, the scores of bullets that would be falling back to the ground at an incredible velocity hopefully missing the innocents that might be tending crops nearby. He forced a smile. "We're here alone, just the two of us, unarmed. Of course we have a drone watching over us in case something goes wrong. Just a few days ago, American soldiers were killed here in this very place. Do you really think they'd send us here without protection?"

Several of the men relaxed slightly at the explanation, but not Jafar. "So, you knew about the attack, about what happened here?"

"Of course."

"Then why would they have sent you here alone?" Jafar jabbed a finger at him. "He's lying!"

Two men rushed forward and grabbed Mo, each by an arm. He didn't struggle. Instead, he focused on remaining calm, waiting for Kane to do something, to do anything.

"Get the American!" shouted someone from behind him.

He glanced over his shoulder to see it was the imam pointing at the SUV. It was approached on either side, people yanking on the door handles to no avail.

"Get the guns!" ordered someone, and several men abandoned the SUV and disappeared inside one of the homes, reemerging with several AK-47s.

Dylan, what are you waiting for?

Kane sat in the SUV, surveying the situation. Right now, it could be a simple misunderstanding. Firing at the drone was the only overtly hostile act that had taken place, and he could dismiss it as the typical distrust that most Afghans had toward foreigners. If he spotted a drone flying over his house for no reason, he'd blow it out of the air too if the law permitted. Everyone valued their privacy.

But the moment they grabbed Mo, everything changed. His head swung from left to right, making note of every potential target, fallback position, and escape route, the latter two already done several times, including when they first arrived.

"Control, Diggler. I'm engaging, over."

"Copy that, Diggler. Backup has been requested. ETA ten minutes, over."

Kane grunted. "This will be long over before they get here." He threw open the door as several men emerged from one of the houses, all sporting AK-47s, all awkwardly held indicating they had little to no experience with the weapons. It made him wonder if these were supplied to the villagers in the attack on the troops earlier in the week, suggesting external involvement.

But it didn't matter. Those holding the guns had reclassified themselves. They were now enemy combatants, and though there were few rules of engagement in his profession, he could freely engage and do whatever was necessary to not only save his own life, but that of his unarmed interpreter.

His left boot hit the ground and he drew the Glock from behind his back, leaving the heavily reinforced door ajar for cover. His right boot pressed into the dirt, as his weapon swung to the left. He fired two rounds into the chest of the man firing at the drone, the only one he was certain knew how to use the weapon, then crouched, leaning out from behind the cover of the door, firing three rapid rounds, one each into the shoulders of the armed men. There was no need to kill them.

Yet.

All three dropped, writhing in agony, their weapons no longer in play. He stepped up onto the SUV's side bar, pushing himself from the ground and aiming his gun over the roof at those holding Mo. In perfect Pashto, he said, "Let him go or die."

Jafar's eyes bulged, perhaps from the threat, perhaps from the revelation that Kane spoke his language.

"Three…two…one…"

The two men holding Mo let go, scurrying backward, their hands held high.

"Get in," said Kane, reaching down and unlocking all four doors. Mo rushed forward, yanking open the passenger side door then climbed inside, slamming it shut and locking it. Kane's weapon was now aimed at Jafar. He flicked the barrel toward the rear door. "Get in."

Jafar's eyes shot wider. "What?"

"I said, get in, or I shoot your imam." He redirected his aim toward the old man.

Jafar thrust his hands in the air, shaking his head. "No! No! I'll go! I'll go!" He stepped forward and climbed in the back.

Kane slowly swung his weapon at those gathered. "He won't be hurt as long as everyone just stays calm. Go back inside your homes now and reflect on what you've done." He lowered into his seat, closed the door, then started the engine as he handed the Glock over to Mo. "If he moves, shoot him."

Mo directed the weapon at Jafar in the back seat. Kane gunned the engine, the vehicle already facing the road out of town, the 180 he had made on arrival intentional. Always position yourself for a quick getaway, if possible. He turned off the traction control, allowing the tires to spin, throwing up rock and dust, obscuring their escape should anyone grow some balls.

He cleared the last of the houses of the village, no balls in evidence. He switched the phone to the SUV's Bluetooth. "Control, Diggler. Any signs of pursuit?"

"Negative, Diggler. Looks like you're clear."

"Copy that, Control. Send in a team to do a sweep of the village. Have them on the look-out for a brown envelope stuffed with a lot of cash last seen on the imam's person."

"Copy that, Diggler. Rapid response team should be there inside of five minutes."

"Copy that, Control. We're going to sit this one out while I have a chat with our guest. Let us know when the village is secure, over."

"Roger that, Diggler. Control, out."

Kane eased the SUV over to the side of the road, reengaging the traction control should he need it. He took the gun back from a nervous Mo, and casually directed it toward Jafar, who sat with his hands up at shoulder height, trembling, his eyes saucers.

"Who are you people?"

Kane shook his head. "I'll be the one asking the questions."

"You lied! You speak our language!"

"And you lied when you invited us into your village as friends."

Jafar appeared mortified at the accusation, his culture demanding anyone invited into their home be treated not only with respect, but as someone they were now responsible for.

"Now, tell me what was in that envelope you handed to your imam?"

Jafar's jaw dropped, and if his eyes could grow any wider, they would have. "I…I don't know what you're talking about."

Kane flipped the gun around then rapped Jafar in the balls with the butt, deciding he shouldn't be the only one with aching boys. Jafar cried out, his hands grabbing for his testicles, and even Mo winced in sympathy. Kane flipped the weapon back. "Now, no more lies, or next time I shoot you in the nuts. What was in the envelope?"

"I can't tell you."

Kane leaned forward and pressed the muzzle of the gun against the hands protecting Jafar's privates. "Last chance. What was in the envelope?"

Jafar closed his eyes, his lower lip trembling. "Money."

Kane smiled slightly. "And where did you get the money?" Jafar said nothing and Kane pressed the gun harder against the man's hands. "Don't stop now. The only way you're surviving this is if you tell me the entire truth."

Jafar sighed. "I don't know his name."

"If you don't know his name, then why is he giving you money?"

"It was payment."

"Payment for what?"

Tears flowed from Jafar's eyes as they opened.

"Payment for what?" repeated Kane.

Jafar shook his head. "No, if I tell you, you'll kill me."

"If you don't tell me, I'll kill you anyway."

Jafar's head drooped. "It was payment for the attack."

Kane exchanged a glance with Mo. "Explain."

Jafar spilled, his words rapid, sounding almost relieved to unburden himself with the truth. "Several weeks ago, a man approached me in the bazaar in Baharak. He made me an offer. He wanted the village to participate in an ambush, and in exchange for each American killed, he would pay us."

"How much did you get?"

"I got one thousand American dollars for each that died."

Kane suppressed his rage. That wasn't a bribe, it was a bounty on the head of every American soldier, and the amount was huge in a country like this. Life-altering. Almost irresistible. "And you agreed to this?"

Jafar shook his head rapidly. "No, not at all! It wasn't my place to commit my village to something like that. I returned home and informed the elders. It was their decision to participate, not mine."

"And your imam that was killed, he agreed?"

"Yes."

Good. The bastard deserved to die.

"If you decided to take the bribe, how did you let the man know?"

"He gave me a phone."

Kane's heart picked up a few beats. "Do you still have it?"

Jafar shook his head. "No, I returned it when I received payment."

"Do you remember the number he had you call?"

Again, Jafar shook his head. "He just showed me how to use something he called speed...something."

"Speed dial?"

"Yes! I never saw a number." Jafar shrugged. "I don't own a phone. I don't know much about them. He showed me how to take pictures with it and how to call him. That's all."

"So, *you* took the photos of the dead soldiers."

Jafar glanced away, the shame evident. "Yes."

"So, tell me how it worked. You made your decision—"

"I didn't. The elders did."

Kane held up a hand. "Fine, the elders made their decision. Then what?"

"I returned to the city and called him, told him when the next meeting with the Americans was, and he said some men would arrive that morning with weapons. They would show us how to use them, and we would set up the ambush outside of town. We had to supply twelve men for the attack."

"Then what happened?"

"Nothing until the day of the meeting. At sunrise, six men arrived. They provided us with weapons and ammunition, and one of them showed us how they worked and explained what would happen. Those involved in the attack hid in the hills. Your men arrived, the meeting was held, but something went wrong and they tried to leave early before we could get in position. The outsiders opened fire and our people did as well. Then when two of your people hid inside the imam's house, the outsiders opened fire on it. Your people were killed, but so were several of ours, including the imam."

Kane struggled to maintain control. He wanted to beat the living shit out of this piece of garbage, then tear off his head and piss in his skull. But he needed information. "Then what happened?"

"As soon as the last American was dead, the new arrivals left without saying anything."

"Did they take the weapons?"

"Some of them, but not all of them. They were in a hurry. I think they knew more Americans were coming."

"And how did they leave?"

"I don't know. They just went into the hills. I assume they had a vehicle somewhere, but I never saw it."

"Were any of them killed?"

"No, only our people. We lost six, including the imam."

"Then what happened?"

"Everybody fled the village and hid in the hills. There are some caves nearby. Your people arrived, then when they left, we returned. I went back to the city, made the phone call, met with the man, he looked at the photos I took, gave me the money, took the phone, and left. I bought some supplies for the village to repair the damage along with all of the roofs, then met you on my way back."

Kane removed the gun from the man's testicles, the story plausible. "Would you recognize the man if you saw him again?"

"I think so."

"And are you willing to help us find him?"

Jafar's face slackened. "If I do, they might attack my village."

"Only if they find out, but I can guarantee you that if you don't help me, your village will be labeled as collaborators."

Jafar stared at him. "What does that mean?"

"It means you won't be eligible for any aid, and no one will come to help you should the Taliban arrive. You'll be on your own. NATO won't help you because of what you did, your own government won't help you, and we'll spread word to the Taliban that you cooperated with us."

Jafar closed his eyes, defeated. "So, I have no choice."

"No. Murderers don't get choices."

"Then I guess I'll help you."

You bet your ass you will.

Kane opened the center console and slid aside a secret panel. He removed a set of comms and inserted the earpiece before activating the system.

And wondered if Langley had a sketch artist who spoke Pashto.

Operations Center 2, CIA Headquarters
Langley, Virginia

Leroux watched as two Black Hawks and an Apache entered the frame, the drone still circling overhead, the gunman failing in his attempt to take it out. The audio from the Rapid Response team leader was being fed directly through to them, playing on the speakers overhead. Something was being said in Pashto and a CIA translator in his ear interpreted.

"He's ordering them to lay down their weapons or they'll be fired upon."

Weapons were tossed to the ground and hands raised. Half a dozen men from the lead chopper rappelled into the village center as the Apache hovered menacingly over the cluster of homes. The second chopper set down at the edge of the village, troops pouring out, a mix of American and Afghan soldiers spreading out in teams of two, conducting house-to-house searches.

"Control, this is Diggler. Status report, over."

Child snickered as he had every time Kane's freshly chosen callsign was used. Though he hadn't the first time. It was one of the senior analysts, twenty years Child's senior, who revealed the source. A quick Google of Boogie Nights and Child was in the loop. And still stuck in it, apparently.

Leroux reactivated his headset. "House-to-house searches are underway. At the rate they're going, assuming no delays, they'll probably be done in ten or fifteen minutes, over."

"Any sign of resistance?"

"Negative, Diggler. Everyone seems to be cooperating."

Kane grunted. "That tends to happen when you have an Apache staring you down. Control, we're going to be staying out of the village with our witness. He's agreed to cooperate. If the villagers ask, tell them he's been taken for interrogation."

"Roger that, Diggler."

"Tell your whiz kid to expect some dates, times, and locations. They're all going to be approximate. I need you to figure out if there is a cellphone that was used at all those times. It could be the one given to our friend here. If we get lucky, it might still be active."

"Roger that, Diggler. We'll get on it as soon as you send us the details."

"Okay, stand by, Control. We'll get you that information in a few minutes. Diggler, out."

Leroux returned his attention to the drone footage, watching as a pile of weapons grew in the village center. When the search was finally over, an Afghan major strode up to an elderly man and patted him down, removing a brown envelope a moment later. He held it up triumphantly toward the eye in the sky, and Leroux smiled as he activated his comms.

"Dragon Heart, this is Control. Confirm the contents of the envelope, over."

"Roger that, Control. Stand by." One of the American soldiers walked over to the Afghan with the envelope. It was handed over then opened. "Control, Dragon Heart Zero-One. Confirmed it's cash. Looks to be at least five grand in US currency, over."

"Copy that, Zero-One."

"Any further special requests, Control?"

"Take photos of all the men, confiscate any automatic weapons, leave their hunting rifles, and make sure that money gets to our asset. He's about two klicks south of your position in an SUV parked on the side of the road, over."

"Roger that, Control. Dragon Heart, out."

Child spun in his chair. "I just got that intel from Kane."

Leroux turned in his chair. "Good. Get to work on it. Pull whatever resources you need. That's your top priority right now."

"Yes, sir."

Leroux's headpiece squawked. "Control, Diggler. Do you happen to have a sketch artist there who speaks Pashto?"

Leroux's eyebrows shot up.

THE MESSENGER

What the hell does he need a sketch artist for?

Wakhan Corridor, Afghanistan

Kane stepped out of the SUV as the Black Hawk hovered overhead. A bag was tossed down to him and he let it hit the ground. He picked it up and opened it, finding the brown envelope in question inside. He waved up at the chopper, giving a thumbs-up, and it banked away, quickly gaining altitude and rejoining the other two helicopters. He climbed into the SUV and started the engine, heading away from the village and toward their next destination. He adjusted the air conditioning to just take the edge off—unless you were truly suffering, it was never wise to create too great a differential between the outside and the inside. A few degrees were enough, otherwise the moment you stepped back outside, you'd be roasting.

He handed the envelope over to Mo. "Count it."

The translator flipped through the bills, and Kane checked his rearview mirror. Jafar was visibly upset. "Five-thousand-six-hundred-

and-twenty," said Mo finally. "Mostly a mix of twenties and fifties, all US dollars."

Kane reached for his phone, now connected to the vehicle's communication system. He tapped a few buttons, launching an app supplied by Langley, then handed the phone to Mo. "Use this. Start taking photos of all the bills. The app will verify that it's not counterfeit and record all the serial numbers, looking for patterns. It'll also upload them to Langley."

Mo's eyes bulged as he stared at the thick stack. "All of them?"

Kane chuckled. "All of them. And just remember what that stack of bills represents. Six American lives. Those serial numbers could lead back to whoever is behind this."

"Isn't it just the Taliban?"

Kane pursed his lips. "It could be and it likely is, but why the payouts? That's completely out of character. Normally, the Taliban would just make contact, tell them what they were going to do, make their demands, then do it. Or, they wouldn't even tell them at all. It just doesn't make sense. And why here? This place is of no strategic importance, especially with the border closed to China."

"What about the other sites? Were they important?"

"Some were, some weren't, but like I said when I briefed you, we can't be sure they're all connected. Some might simply have been regular attacks, just in unusual areas."

"What about the one where they were taking photos?"

"Strategically unimportant."

"What does that tell you?"

Kane paused for a moment, slowing as he approached a missing part of the road. "If I wanted to create instability, this would be one way to do it. Make the entire country appear unsecured, and perhaps NATO doesn't pull out so quickly."

"But why would the Taliban do that? It's to their advantage for NATO to leave."

"Maybe it's not the Taliban."

Kane glanced in the rearview mirror, having forgotten he was still speaking in Pashto, many of his conversations with Mo in the man's native language so that Kane could keep up his skills. "What do you mean?" he asked Jafar.

Jafar looked away, as if remembering he wasn't part of the team. He was their prisoner.

Kane accelerated as they cleared the destroyed portion of the road where an IED had clearly gone off at some point. "Listen, Jafar, the sooner we have our answers, the sooner you can go home, and if there's a chance this isn't the Taliban, we need to know that. Why did you say what you did? This could help you and your people."

Jafar stared at his hands as he wrung them. "It's just that I have my suspicions that the men that arrived in our village that morning weren't Afghan."

Kane's eyebrow shot up as he exchanged a surprised look with Mo. "What makes you say that?"

"Well, only one of them spoke. He was definitely Afghan, but the others said nothing, at least to any of my people. But when they were rushing down the hillside into the village, one of them tripped and cursed in a language I didn't recognize."

Kane's foot eased off the accelerator as his mind became distracted. "And you have no idea what language it was?"

Jafar shook his head.

"Could it have been English, Russian, Chinese?"

Jafar shrugged. "No idea. I speak Pashto and Dari. I think I heard Chinese when I was younger, but I wouldn't know."

"These other men who didn't speak, did they look Afghan?"

"Oh, yes. To me, they appeared true Taliban, and if it weren't for the man cursing, I never would have suspected anything. And at the time, I didn't, not until you two started talking."

Kane chewed his cheek for a moment as he pressed harder on the accelerator. He had a rendezvous to keep at a small airstrip where a plane would be waiting to take them to their next destination, but this new bit of intel could be a bombshell. He motioned toward the bills forgotten in Mo's hand, switching to English. "Get to work on those. I'm going to contact Control. Somebody needs to start looking into our friend's idea."

Operations Center 2, CIA Headquarters
Langley, Virginia

"The serial numbers are starting to come in," announced Tong.

Leroux turned his chair to face her. "Start running them, see if we can find out any history on them, what bank first received them, were any of them reported stolen, anything that might give us an idea where they came from."

"We're on it," replied Tong.

The speakers overhead squelched. "Control, Diggler. Come in, over."

Leroux adjusted his headset and tapped the button to accept the communication. "Diggler, Control. Go ahead, over."

"Our friend has suggested an interesting possibility. He says he believes at least some of the people who arrived in his village the morning of the attack may not have been from Afghanistan. They may have actually been foreigners, despite looking the part."

Leroux leaned back in his chair, turning it to take in the room, everyone momentarily distracted from their duties. If it weren't the Taliban or some other local terrorist group, then who the hell was it? Why would there be foreign combatants in Afghanistan?

Then something occurred to him. "Diggler, are we certain it's not just other Muslim fundamentalists from around the world joining the cause?"

"No, Control, we're *not* sure. Anything's possible with these people. Like we saw with ISIS, we were fighting American citizens. Just cast a broader net in your search. See if you get lucky on piecing together some of their faces. According to our contact, they would be the ones firing on the imam's home."

"Roger that, Diggler. We'll get right on it." He checked a display showing the projected ETA for Kane at his rendezvous point. He had about five minutes to spare in a two-hour drive. "Diggler, you'd better get a wiggle on. We don't want Shaw's of London to get a bad reputation for holding up flights."

Kane chuckled. "As long as Shaw's is paying for my speeding tickets, we should be fine. Diggler, out."

The entrance to the operations center opened with a beep and a hiss, Director Morrison stepping inside. Normally, the man received his updates electronically. Whenever he did show up, it meant he either had a personal interest, concern for one of his people, or someone from Washington on his back.

He was guessing the latter.

He rose. "Hey, Chief, how can we help you?"

"If anyone's got a crowbar, maybe they can help pry Washington off my ass. The moment you confirmed there were payouts for the death of American troops, the Pentagon went ape-shit crazy. They want to know who is behind this, and then eliminate them publicly so nobody ever gets the idea of doing this again. Incentivizing people to kill our troops can never be tolerated."

"We're working on it, Chief. Kane just reported a few moments ago that their local contact believes the men that arrived to direct the attack might not have been from Afghanistan. Kane's also sending us all the serial numbers on the bills that were recovered. We're also looking for a pattern in the phone calls made in Baharak to see if we can track the phone that might have been used to coordinate the pay-off. And Kane requested a sketch artist to put together a composite of the man who made the payout."

Morrison's head bobbed with satisfaction the entire time. "Anything I can do to help?"

Leroux smirked. "Keep Washington on your ass and not ours?"

Morrison roared with laughter and slapped Leroux on the shoulder. "I'll do my best, son, I'll do my best." He headed toward the door, throwing his hand up in the air, giving the team a quick wave. "Excellent work, people, keep it up!"

The door was about to hiss shut when it reopened and an awkward looking man stumbled in.

"Did someone request a sketch artist that speaks Pashto?"

Leroux/White Residence, Fairfax Towers
Falls Church, Virginia

Leroux yawned as he stepped inside the apartment he shared with the love of his life, Sherrie White. The giggling he had heard on the other side of the door fell silent and a head poked around the corner as Sherrie leaned over on the couch.

"Hey, sweetie. Keep that thing in your pants. We've got company."

Leroux chuckled. "It wouldn't matter. I'm too tired." He kicked his shoes off and stepped into the living area to see Lee Fang, her legs curled up under her on the other end of the couch, a glass of white wine in her hand. Sherrie rose and gave him a kiss that had him rethinking his previous statement before she finally broke away.

"I missed you," she whispered.

"Me too."

She tilted her head toward the bottle on the table. "Can I pour you a glass?"

He waved it off. "No, I'm going straight to bed after I have a shower."

"Want us to join you?"

Leroux's eyes shot wide and he glanced at their guest, the sultry look on Fang's face forcing them even wider. "Huh?"

Sherrie roared in laughter and Fang joined in. "Oh, dear, you should see your face." She patted his cheek. "You couldn't handle both of us. Go take your shower, then get your rest. We'll try to keep it down."

"Perhaps I should leave," said Fang, putting her glass on the table.

Leroux held up a hand, stopping her. "No, don't worry about it. I'm just going to have the smart speaker play white noise and I'll be out like a light. You two have fun."

Sherrie leaned in and grabbed him by the ass. "Wake up half an hour early, and *we* can have a little fun."

Something down below declared its vote in favor of her suggestion. "We'll see," he said. "But I could get called back at any minute."

She gave him a peck, releasing the grip she had on his ass. "Then you better get to bed."

He headed toward the bathroom, then glanced back at Fang. "Oh, Dylan says hi."

She smiled. "If you get a chance, say hi back, and ask him how his balls are doing."

Sherrie snorted.

He blocked any more information with his hand. "I still don't want to know what the hell you two are talking about."

"She shot him in the nuts because he shot her in the twins," explained Sherrie, with a touch of indignation. She threw a finger toward Fang. "Show him."

Fang rose and grabbed the bottom of her shirt, sending Leroux running from the room, the two girls cackling behind him. He stripped out of the clothes he had been wearing for two days then climbed into the shower, leaning his forehead against the tile as he let the hot water run over his exhausted body. He finally pushed off the wall with his hands then washed, the occasional laugh or excited utterance heard from the two women.

And he smiled.

He couldn't believe how good his life was. It wasn't that it was necessarily that much better than most people's, it was just that it was far better than anything he had imagined for himself. He had been certain his life would be spent alone, split between a generic cubicle and an apartment bereft of any signs of a life well lived.

But then he had met Sherrie, and everything had changed. He thanked God every day that Director Morrison had used her to test his loyalty with a honeypot trap. It had broken his heart when he found out the truth, but thanks to Kane who forced them back together, they were now a couple. This was the woman he was going to marry. This was the woman he intended to spend the rest of his life with.

Assuming her job as a CIA operative didn't get her killed.

He shut off the shower, toweled dry, then climbed into bed, setting the alarm on his phone. Sherrie giggled on the other side of the wall and he told his smart speaker to play white noise, the static immediately blocking out most of the sounds of life around him. He closed his eyes, fitting a sleeping mask in place, blocking out the early evening sun forcing its way around the edges of the blackout curtains.

Sherrie's laughter broke through the static and he smiled. He loved her laugh. He loved everything about her. He loved…

He lifted the mask and grabbed his phone, bringing up the alarm. He flicked his thumb, shaving 30 minutes from its previous setting, then lay back down, looking forward to that half-hour as he drifted off to sleep.

Outside Kunduz, Afghanistan

Kane climbed out of the small charter with his carry-on, then waited for Jafar and Mo to join him on the dirt tarmac as the propellers of the charter plane came to a rest. A pre-arranged SUV, much like the one they had left behind at their rendezvous point, sat waiting for them.

The pilot, an Aussie named Ben Ledger, stepped out and Kane shook the man's hand. "Thanks for getting us here in one piece."

"No worries, mate. Life has enough dramas. You don't need to add worrying about your plane falling out of the sky to it."

Kane laughed and slapped the man on the shoulder. "We'll see you in eight hours."

"Copy that, mate."

Kane tossed his bag in the back seat then climbed into the driver's seat and closed the door, noting its weight, confirming the vehicle was reinforced. He started the engine then pulled away, and within minutes the airport, if it could be called that, was lost in the distance. When they were out of sight of any prying eyes that might have been watching the area, he lifted up the center console and slid aside a secret panel, a Glock revealed along with several spare mags. He left them in place for the moment, then checked ahead to make sure the road was straight.

"Take the wheel," he said to Mo.

Mo's eyes flared slightly but he had learned not to question anything Kane said, and grabbed the wheel as Kane turned his attention to his phone. It had taken two hours to reach the rendezvous with the plane, then another half-dozen to get them where they were now, several stops made along the way to pick up and drop off other passengers. Yes, he could have the military transporting him, but he was still using his cover, and he didn't want some look-out spotting him climbing out of a military chopper and radioing ahead to their destination, warning them he wasn't actually a civilian.

He raced through the updates in his secure messenger. The team back in Langley had taken advantage of his travel time, switching shifts to get some rest. He preferred to have Leroux and his team on the job, but no matter how good someone was, they could be rendered useless if exhausted. Nothing so far had shown up with the recovered bills that raised any red flags, and they had nothing yet on the sketch of the money man Jafar had spent the two-hour drive putting together with the artist before boarding the plane. It was a good likeness, but unfortunately, a face with a heavy beard wrapped in a keffiyeh didn't leave much room for many distinguishing details. They would have to rely on Jafar identifying the man should they find him.

The only signs of progress were that they might have found a match to the telephone number. The analysis continued, but they had found one used in two of the three instances in question, and were working on the third. Langley analysts were still attempting to piece together frames and footage from the drone, hoping to assemble a full face they might put through the databases for a match. If they could confirm the identity of just one of the suspected foreign hostiles, it could break the investigation wide open.

He fired off a message to Langley informing them they were safely on the ground, heading toward their destination, and that he was off comms. If they needed him, they would signal him through his watch and he would put the gear in place.

He handed his phone over to Mo. "Finish getting those serial numbers in. I still think that could be key."

"You got it." Mo fished the wad of bills from his inside pocket and returned to the tedious task.

Their next destination was a three-hour drive through what should be safe territory, or as safe as you could expect in Afghanistan. And at their destination was a man with a bunch of expensive new toys, including a shiny broken-down British automobile.

A man in desperate need of insurance.

Operations Center 2, CIA Headquarters
Langley, Virginia

Leroux entered the operations center with a spring in his step and a smile he couldn't hide no matter how hard he tried. Sacrificing thirty minutes of sleep was the best damn decision he had made all week. God, he loved that woman. "Good morning, everyone!" he said with a wave. A mix of greetings were returned, and Tong flashed a smile at him.

"Good morning."

And he could swear she sounded slightly hurt. He was fully aware she was attracted to him, but he had hoped that she had moved on from those feelings he couldn't possibly return. His delirious happiness had to be hard on her. He had always assumed it was easier for women to get a boyfriend. All they had to do was ask. After all, when he was single and lonely, holed up in his apartment, if anyone had come up to him and asked him out, he'd have leaped at the opportunity.

Though maybe his loneliness had nothing to do with lack of opportunity, and everything to do with the fact he had been painfully shy, insecure, and awkward. The only reason he was with a woman like Sherrie, someone so vivacious and outgoing, so confident in her sexuality, her abilities, her intelligence, was because the job had forced them together. If it weren't for her, he'd be as alone as Tong was.

From casual conversation, he was aware her typical Friday night was spent alone, at home, as forlorn as he once was. Perhaps it wasn't easier for women. It required courage to ask someone out, whether you were a man or a woman. He felt for her, and wished there were something he could do, though what that might be, he had no idea.

Date the two of them.

He suppressed a chuckle. In today's society, it wouldn't actually be out of the question.

"You couldn't handle both of us."

Sherrie's words from last night echoed in his head. She was right. He had a hard enough time keeping up with one woman, let alone two.

And never mind the bedroom.

"Are you okay?"

He flinched then noticed Tong staring at him. "Huh?"

"Well, you've just been standing there with a weird smile on your face."

Leroux's cheeks flushed and he continued to his workstation. "Sorry, just something that happened last night."

"What?"

She called your bluff.

He dropped his bag on top of his desk. "You had to be there." He thought he needed to provide a little more. "We had company. Or rather, Sherrie had company." He thought back at the jokes made at his expense, and he smiled again, shaking his head. "I don't think I'll ever understand women."

Child spun in his chair. "Preach, brother. I've never been able to figure them out."

"Maybe that's because the last woman you—"

Leroux held up a hand, cutting off Mark Therrien from delivering what would no doubt be a zinger at Child's expense. "Okay, before this descends into madness, did the night shift get us anything useful?"

Tong nodded. "We've got a face."

Leroux sat in his chair. "One of the gunmen?"

"Yup." She pointed at the displays dominating the front of the room, and an image was shown, half a dozen segments pieced together, enough for the facial recognition software to work with. The man sported a keffiyeh with a thick beard, dark complexion, and if it weren't for a jagged scar on his left cheek, he could be the man from Jafar's sketch. In other words, the man appeared as Afghan as any other.

He chewed his cheek for a moment. "And Jafar thinks these guys are foreigners?"

Tong shrugged. "From Kane's report, it was only because he heard one of them say something in a language he didn't understand."

"Any hits yet?"

116

"Not yet, but they just started the database search at the end of their shift. Hopefully, we'll get lucky."

"Anything on those bills yet?"

"Let me check." Child tapped at his keyboard, then his eyes shot wide. "Now, this is interesting." Everyone turned to face the young analyst, but he said nothing else as he continued to stare at his screen.

Therrien finally threw his hands in the air. "Well, you can't leave us hanging like that!"

Child looked up. "Huh? Oh, sorry. We just got the last of the bills, and according to the Fed's database, over eighty percent of them were first delivered to European banks."

Tong frowned, Child's report disappointing in its unimportance. "What's so unusual about that? We know the Taliban and their ilk are spread throughout Europe and Asia, more so than they are here. If they're going to get their hands on lump sums of American cash, then they're more likely to get it at an ATM in Berlin than they are in New York."

Leroux had to agree, though Child's smug expression suggested he didn't. "If you had let me finish, you might not be eating those words. You would have heard me say that all the bills in this particular stack of cash came from six different banks, all in the same batches."

Leroux's eyes narrowed. "What do you mean?"

"I mean, it looks like somebody went to six different banks and withdrew roughly a thousand bucks."

"So, what are you saying?" asked Tong.

"I'm saying, somebody went and took money from six different banks, and, based upon when these bills were issued, I'd say it all happened within the same week, three months ago."

Leroux's head bobbed. "So, it's not just a mix of bills that they accumulated over time, robbing people, knocking over street vendors."

"No. These were proper withdrawals, made from a bank or an ATM, all in Europe."

"And then, four weeks later, we have our first attack that we think could be linked, and a couple of weeks later, we have our first attack where we spotted the cameraman." Leroux pursed his lips. "Coincidence?"

Tong regarded him. "I didn't think you believed in it."

Leroux shook his head. "I don't. I think we're on to something here. This isn't something pulled together by a ragtag group. This is a group with connections, well organized, and at least reasonably well funded."

Child eyed him. "Six grand isn't exactly well funded."

Leroux turned to face him. "You're forgetting that that was the seventh attack that we think is related. Over thirty of our people are dead. If the bounty was the same in all these attacks, that's at least thirty grand. That's a huge amount of money for a group that's based in Afghanistan."

Child grunted. "You must get paid a hell of a lot more than I do because that's huge to me too."

Leroux chuckled. "Yes, but put it in perspective. The typical American makes about fifty grand a year, and the average Afghan

118

makes about a grand. That's a fifty-fold difference. If whoever is behind this is paying a grand a head, remember that's a grand to us based upon the lifestyle we're accustomed to. For them, that's equivalent to fifty thousand dollars a head. That's life-altering. And when you're talking five or six or more per incident, it's an incredible sum of money, more than enough to take care of one man and his family for quite a while in a country like that."

Tong's head slowly bobbed. "Or enough to help an entire village."

Leroux stabbed a finger at her. "Exactly. We've been wondering why they would participate, and that could be our answer. It's simply too much money for them to pass up, especially in a country that doesn't value life as we do, and certainly doesn't value foreigners' lives. I'm not saying they jumped at it without serious thought, but the offer of unprecedented cash and noninterference in a country where almost all the troops providing meaningful security are about to leave, they probably weighed their options and the money won out. I'm not going to judge them by our standards, but I am going to judge those behind this."

"Thirty thousand for so many lives? A thousand to kill someone? It's ridiculous! It's disgusting!" spat Child. "Who places so little value on a human life, especially on people that have been helping them for years?"

"A grand might mean nothing to us, but to them, it's equivalent to fifty. And when you've known nothing but war, nothing but struggle, then perhaps it proves to be too big a temptation."

"It obviously did," muttered Child. "I don't care how much anybody offered me, I wouldn't kill any of you. Except maybe Mark."

"Love you too, Randy," shouted Therrien from the back, two birds on full display. Everyone chuckled, the tension reliever desperately needed.

Leroux smacked his hands together. "Let's keep tracking this money, see if any other bills from the same batches have reentered the system in the past two months. We might be able to track the path it took to get into the country. And let's see if we can put together some more faces from the footage we've got. Also, let's start pulling satellite and drone footage from the region before and after the attacks. Jafar said he didn't see how they left, but they had to have some mode of transport. We might get lucky and pick something up. We need to find out who the hell is behind this before there's another ambush."

En Route to Cheyabi, Afghanistan

Kane guided them toward the village, now less than an hour away. Jafar sat silently in the back seat, resigned to his fate, as Mo flipped through frame grabs taken from the drone footage showing their next target. He held up the tablet showing the British luxury SUV with its hood open.

"How much does one of these cost?"

Kane glanced at the image for a moment. "More than you and I make."

Mo grunted. "Something tells me you make a lot more than I do."

Kane chuckled. "I wouldn't be so sure about that. They give us big expense accounts for our covers, but my paycheck at the end of the day that I have to live off of in the real world is adequate, but nothing that would buy me a car like that."

"So, you make less than six thousand a year?"

Kane's eyebrows shot up. "Huh?"

"Well, if everyone's getting a thousand dollars per American death, and six men died in this attack a couple of months ago, then doesn't that mean the man received six thousand dollars?"

Kane eased his foot off the accelerator, not willing to use the cruise control on roads where you might have to react in an instant, and cursed at not having made the connection. He had been thinking of the payoffs in Western terms. He had been focusing on the fact there were payoffs made, not the amounts of those payments. Yes, a village receiving $6,000 in Afghanistan was significant in a country so poor, but an $80,000 automobile in the United States was still $80,000 in Afghanistan, and there weren't any dealerships here. It would have been imported. Yes, that likely meant the disabled car was stolen, its previous owner, perhaps in the Carolinas, still mourning the loss. But there was no way $6,000 bought a stolen luxury British automobile and all the other extravagances evident in the photograph.

$60,000 perhaps, but not $6,000.

Maybe this guy negotiated a better deal than Jafar.

He glanced in the rearview mirror at Jafar, switching to Pashto. "Did you negotiate the amount?"

Jafar's eyes narrowed. "What do you mean?"

"A thousand per American soldier's life. Did you negotiate that amount, or did he just tell you that's what it was?"

"He just told me. He said he'd give me one thousand for each photo of a dead American I provided."

Kane sighed heavily, shaking his head. "So little money for so many innocent lives." He looked back once again at Jafar. "How big a difference does six thousand dollars make in the lives of your village to warrant murder?"

Jafar shook his head. "You don't understand. That six thousand was for me, not the village."

Kane took his foot off the gas. "But you gave it to the imam."

"Yes, because I didn't feel I deserved it. It should be shared by the village."

"But I thought you said the village elders approved this plan?"

"They did."

"And they approved it, knowing that the six grand was being given to you, not the village?"

Jafar shook his head. "No, you don't understand. The six thousand was meant for me, but I didn't feel I deserved to keep it, so I gave it to the imam. The village was paid sixty-thousand."

Kane hit the brakes, bringing them to a rapid halt on the side of the road. He put the vehicle in park and twisted in his seat, staring directly at Jafar. "You mean the payout wasn't six thousand to the village? It was six to you, plus another sixty?"

Jafar nodded.

"Then why the hell didn't you tell us that?"

Jafar averted his eyes. "You never asked. And if I told you, the village would lose its money and all of this would have been for nothing."

Kane cursed, fishing his comms out of the center console. He shook his head at Mo as he fit the gear in place. "This changes everything. Funding like that isn't local. It's not grassroots. Something bigger is going on here."

Operations Center 2, CIA Headquarters

Langley, Virginia

Leroux flipped through the partial images of the other gunmen that had opened fire on the imam's home, marking them as outsiders. Unfortunately, there just wasn't enough to work with—a quarter of a face, a third. The computer could guess on some of them, though the number of false positives could prove overwhelming.

It would be guilt by association. They had one target with a full face pieced together. Identify him, and perhaps there might be known associates on file they could match up with the others. The likelihood was they wouldn't find any of them in their files. He could be from Pakistan, Syria, or Brooklyn. There was no way to know, though if he were American or from some other Western ally, he might have traveled on a passport, so his photo would be in the system.

Right now, they were working with little to no information, beyond the fact bounties were being paid. They had no idea who was paying it beyond a vague sketch, who was paying that person, or even the purpose behind it beyond killing Americans.

The comms squawked overhead. "Control, this is Diggler. Come in, over."

Leroux snatched his headset, fitting it in place, detecting the urgency in his friend's voice. "This is Control. Go ahead, Diggler."

"We've got new intel. It turns out our friend was holding out on us. The thousand dollars per head was a bonus to him personally. The village itself received ten thousand a head."

Leroux's heart raced as he turned in his chair. Everyone in the room was stunned, especially after discussing what $1,000 meant to someone in Afghanistan compared to the United States. $10,000 changed the equation entirely. "Then where is the rest of the money? You said there was less than six thousand in the envelope."

"There was. He handed the envelope over to his imam because he felt he didn't deserve it. He used it to buy supplies for the village, then donated the rest. Apparently, the remaining sixty was in his vehicle."

Leroux collapsed back in his chair, staring into the distance as he processed this new information. It explained a lot, like why a village was willing to murder American soldiers who had never done anything but help them. $60,000 was an astronomical amount in a country like that. But it changed the equation the other way as well. They had been searching for somebody who had supplied at least $30,000, now they were after somebody who supplied hundreds of thousands. A much different sum. $30,000 pulled together, over multiple withdraws was far easier than over ten times that. And with no signs of these attacks letting up, it could be the tip of the iceberg.

"Are we sure about this?" he finally asked.

"He has no reason to lie, and look at where we're headed. Our target has a shiny new nightmare on four wheels, satellite dishes, new roof, new everything. Six grand doesn't buy that, but sixty-six does."

"So, what's your plan?"

"I'm going to lean a lot harder on this guy than I did Jafar. We need answers. With these dollar amounts, this is bigger than we thought, and the players might be as well."

"Agreed," said Leroux. "I'm going to recommend we go back into the last village and search for that money. The serial numbers might provide us with more information."

"Copy that, Control. Keep me posted. Our ETA is thirty minutes to the next target."

"Copy that, Diggler. Control, out." Leroux disconnected and turned to the room of highly experienced analysts. "This changes the scope of things. Let's see if we can figure out how close together the withdrawals were made geographically and timewise. It might give us an indication as to how many people are involved. If things are happening close together but far apart, we have to assume this isn't a couple of people withdrawing small donations from supporters around the world. This is something bigger with funding that goes beyond what we thought. Start pulling banking transactions as well where we have taps. See if we can find anything in common like wire transfers arriving at multiple banks from the same source. Any type of pattern that might identify where the money came from and who withdrew it."

"We're on it, boss," said Tong.

Leroux rose. "I'm going to go brief the Chief. This new intel could change everything."

Cheyabi, Afghanistan

Firash relaxed in his above-ground pool without a care in the world as the sun baked him. He now floated in more water than he had ever seen in person outside of a river or lake. It was luxurious. It was something he had only seen in pictures. A dream beyond reach. But the moment the offer had been presented to him, it was the first thing he could picture purchasing with the promised bounty.

He just wished he lived somewhere he could truly enjoy it.

In America, he had no doubt a pool like this and a fancy car—if he could get it to work—would have women fawning over him non-stop. But Afghanistan was far too conservative a country for that. Perhaps in Kabul, he might attract some questionable women, especially foreign women, but not here in the middle of nowhere.

For now, he'd be content to enjoy the fruits of very little labor. All he had done was gather a dozen of his friends, promised them each $500, then took photos of the aftermath. He didn't care about the

Americans. As far as he was concerned, they were no different than the Russians, though he could honestly say he had never met a Russian. They had been forced out long before he was born. But as far as he was concerned, they were all the same. Foreign invaders. Yes, things had improved, but they were rapidly worsening, and nobody believed that the central government would maintain control after the foreigners left. So he had snatched his opportunity, and for the past several weeks, was living an unbelievable life.

He just wished the damn SUV worked.

He was happy, his friends were happy, and the community was happy when he bought the mosque a new truck. The entire event had gone so smoothly, it had been almost easy. The ambush had been set up outside of town, and when the Americans left, those he had hired for the job had merely opened fire with the weapons provided by the others that had arrived that morning. The strangers did most of the work. They fired the rockets, they threw the grenades. If anyone from his village had killed an American, it was purely by luck.

But it didn't matter where the bullets came from—he was paid for every photo. It was so easy. When he collected his money, he offered his services for any future jobs. His contact had been non-committal, but said he would reach out should an opportunity arise. He hadn't heard from him and was tempted to call the man himself. What his contact didn't realize when explaining how to use the phone given to coordinate the mission, was that he was fully aware of how to use it. He loved tech, and was in charge of the village's satellite phone.

He knew what he was doing, so pulling the phone number from the speed dial setting was easy—a fact he kept to himself when returning the phone after being paid. And because he had done that, it meant he could reach out himself. With the Americans soon pulling out, there wouldn't be many more opportunities to earn this type of money, perhaps for the rest of his life.

He eyed through the rear door the satellite phone charging on a table inside. The urge to call was overwhelming. Little of the money was left, and as he had already discovered, the Western lifestyle required money to maintain it. He growled at his misfortune with the SUV.

There was a knock at the front door. He climbed out of the pool, toweled off, then threw on a robe as whoever it was knocked again. "I'm coming! Give me a moment!" He rushed through the living area, unable to hold back his grin at the 65-inch flat-screen powered by the new solar panels with content fed by the new satellite dishes on his roof, with entertainment from all around the world—including pornography, something he had only heard of but had never seen. The television had revealed a world to him he hadn't known existed. It was wondrous, confusing, terrifying.

And he wasn't certain he wanted to be part of it.

Life was simple here, but hard. Until a couple of weeks ago, it was the only life he knew, and now that he was aware of how much better it was in the rest of the world, he wasn't sure he was happy with his own reality. The novelties he had bought with the one-time windfall he was meant to share with his village, but instead kept for himself, certainly were helping him forget his current plight, but as he had already discovered with the car, these things would break in time, then he'd be left where he was previously—a poor man in a poor country, though this time with a taste of what life could be.

The veil that had hidden the world outside was now lifted away.

Permanently.

He opened the door and his heart leaped into his throat at the sight of a white man standing there, smiling broadly, with an Afghan behind him.

"Hi there. My name is Dylan Kane. I represent Shaw's of London. It's an insurance company. Do you know what insurance is?" the man asked in what he assumed was English, the other one translating.

Firash said nothing, still stunned at the situation. He couldn't recall a white person being in his village that wasn't either a soldier, or accompanied by them. He finally shook his head as he realized the question was left dangling, unanswered.

"Well, insurance is designed to protect your valuables, like that fancy car and the TV I can see down the hall."

Firash's eyes shot wide, a possible solution to his problem being presented. "So, if something breaks, you'll fix it?"

The man smiled broadly at the translation. "Stolen, broken, damaged, anything. You simply pay a small monthly fee, and if something happens, you let us know and we take care of it. Like that car you've got there. Judging by the make, I assume it's not working?"

Firash muttered a curse. "It worked for three days."

Kane laughed. "I'm sorry to hear that, my friend, but if you agree to go with our insurance, I'll write it up so that it says the car was in perfect working order. Then you just wait a few weeks, call us and tell us there's something wrong with the car, and my company will take care of everything. May we come in to discuss it?"

Firash rapidly agreed, stepping aside, and the two men entered. He closed the door and turned to face them when Kane's hand darted out and grabbed him by the throat, squeezing with a grip unlike anything he had ever thought possible.

And then in perfect Pashto, the man said, "You and I are going to have a little talk, and if I don't feel you're telling me the truth, your friends are going to find you drowned in your fancy pool."

Firash grabbed at Kane's hand, struggling to remove it from around his throat, to no avail.

"Do you understand the position you're in?"

Firash nodded, his eyes filling with tears as he slowly grew faint. Kane eased up slightly on his grip, then hauled him down the hallway before shoving him into a chair. The translator bound his hands behind his back, leaving him completely at the mercy of this crazed American.

Kane pulled another chair closer and sat in front of him, staring directly at him. "What's your name?"

"F-Firash."

"Do you know why we're here?"

Firash knew. Of course he knew. He wasn't a fool. "No."

Kane smacked him across the cheek, the sting in some way worse than a punch, for there was an element of humiliation to it. You punched a man. You slapped a woman. And Kane's action emasculated him.

"I'll ask you again, or we're going to conduct this interrogation in your pool. Do you know why we're here?"

Firash closed his eyes. "Yes."

"Good, but just so we're clear, you tell me why we're here."

Firash's shoulders slumped. This would be his punishment for participating in the deaths of the infidels, for once he revealed the truth, there was no way they were letting him live. But at least he would die a martyr, and his eternity in Jannah would be the bliss all good Muslims lived their lives in service for. "You're here because of what happened," he finally said.

"And what happened?"

"The American soldiers were killed."

"Exactly. Tell us everything, and you live, and we won't even take away your toys."

Firash's eyes shot wide at the prospect of surviving the day, and told them everything about being approached in the market by a man who offered his village $10,000 per dead soldier, plus a $1000 bonus to him personally. He had asked if it were necessary to give the money to the village, and was told what he did with the money was up to him. He could share it with his community, his friends, or keep it for himself, but he had to supply a dozen men willing to fight, and perhaps die. He hadn't any concept of how much money that was, but there was no doubt it was an enormous amount, something that would change his life for the better.

And he had indicated his interest.

The man had given him a cellphone, explained how to use it, and told him to call when a decision was made. He had gone home, talked to a group of friends, and offered them a pittance, though the amount was still more than any of them had seen in their lifetimes. An agreement had been reached, and it had been far easier than he would have thought. The Americans had never done anything to hurt them, and if anything, had only helped them, but they were leaving. And everybody wanted to be on the right side of the Taliban, and helping them while getting payouts was a win-win for everyone.

Except of course, for the Americans.

He had made the call, agreed to the terms, and provided the date and time of the next American visit. Six Taliban had arrived that morning, showed them the weapons, coordinated the attack, then disappeared the moment the last shot was fired. He took his photos, then everyone returned to the village, keeping their mouths shut. Two days later, he met with the man, received his payment, and was told that if anyone asked him about the money, to say he found it in a government convoy that had been attacked.

And he hadn't heard from the man since.

Kane pulled a tablet computer out of his satchel, then tapped on it several times, bringing up a drawing of a man. He held it up for Firash to see. "Is this the man you met?"

Firash stared at the drawing. "It does look like him, though I couldn't really say one way or the other, except to say that it's definitely not *not* him."

Kane frowned, apparently not pleased with his response.

"I have a picture of him if you want."

Kane's eyes widened and the translator's jaw dropped. "How the hell did you get a photo of him?"

"The village has a satellite phone so whoever is driving the truck into town for supplies takes it, just in case. So, when I went to collect my pay-out, I used it to take a photo of him when he was approaching, just in case if I ever got caught, I could perhaps bargain for my freedom."

Kane leaned back and chuckled. "You might just have saved your ass a good beating. Where is this photo?"

"It's still on the phone."

"And where's the phone?"

He jerked his chin at a table against the wall, a satellite phone sitting on top, charging with the only electricity in the village. The translator stepped over to the table and unplugged the phone, handing it to Kane. He worked it expertly, then held it up, showing the photo in question.

"Is this him?"

Firash nodded, his heart hammering with the realization he had just betrayed the Taliban. If they found out, not only would he die, but it would be a horribly painful death, and could mean the end for his entire village.

"Do you have a name for him?"

"No, I know nothing of him."

"The phone he gave you, where is it?"

"He took it back when he paid me."

"And the number that he had you call?"

This was a lie he had to tell. He could lie to the Taliban about the photo, say that the American had shown it to him, not that he had taken it, but there was no way to explain the phone number. "It was programmed into the phone. I have no idea what it was."

Kane appeared satisfied with this and handed the phone back to his translator, then passed him the tablet that had been sitting on his lap. "Copy the photo onto this."

The traitor to his country perched on a window ledge and went to work as Kane leaned forward.

"Is there anything else you can tell me?"

Firash shook his head. "No, I don't think so."

"What about the men that arrived that morning? Anything about them?"

Another shake of the head.

"You didn't take any photos?"

"No."

"Did you speak to any of them?"

Firash thought for a moment. "To one of them, yes. He explained what would happen and showed us how to work the weapons."

"What about the others?"

"No. They mostly kept to themselves."

"Did you hear them say anything to each other?"

Firash's eyes narrowed. "I don't think so, but they must have. I guess I just didn't notice."

"So, you didn't hear them speak Pashto or another language?"

His eyes narrowed further. "Another language?"

Kane finally came out and asked the question directly. "Did you get the impression that any of them weren't from Afghanistan?"

Firash's jaw dropped and he leaned back. Just the mere suggestion had his mind racing, and it flashed back to the day of the attack. His assignment was to take the photos only, to be the liaison, so he hadn't been involved in the shooting, but his friends had, and they had all been shouting instructions to each other, the heat of the battle intense despite lasting less than ten minutes. But as he pictured what had happened, as he replayed the events in his head, he realized the Taliban had said nothing during the entire firefight.

His jaw slackened at a memory. "They used hand signals!"

"What?"

He stared at Kane. "They never said anything, but they used hand signals during the fight."

Kane's head bobbed slowly. "Interesting."

As his captor scratched his chin, Firash wondered what the man was thinking. This was obviously an American spy. What did the use of hand signals mean? Why was he so curious about whether the outsiders had spoken? His own curiosity won out. "Why is this important?" he asked.

Kane ignored him, instead abruptly rising and turning to the translator, saying something in English. The translator packed up his equipment, leaving the satphone charging before cutting the bindings free.

Firash rubbed his wrists. "What are you going to do to me?"

"Nothing," said Kane. "I'm not here to deliver justice for what you did." Firash's shoulders slumped in relief and he wisely, he thought, kept his mouth shut. Kane headed for the door. "What I am going to do, however, is put the word out that you were very cooperative. Too bad you have no way of reaching your friend to let him know that it's a lie." Kane swirled his finger at his surroundings. "Enjoy this while you can. I don't think you'll be alive to enjoy it for much longer."

Every muscle slackened in Firash's body, and shame swept through him as urine ran down his leg, puddling on the floor at his feet.

Kane smirked at the sight. "You have a nice day now."

He and the traitor left, the door slamming shut, and his entire body shook as he thanked Allah that his brother had taken the family into the city to shop, otherwise they would be witness to his shame. He stared at the television, the screen black, and his mind drifted inexplicably to the nonsensical. He was two seasons into Breaking Bad and he had to know how it finished.

But he could be dead before the day was through.

He forced himself to focus through his panic. The man who had paid him had warned him not to tell anyone anything, and yet the only thing he hadn't shared was the fact he had the telephone number. His eyes shot wide and he leaped from his chair, his foot slipping in the puddle of urine, taking him down to a knee. It twisted painfully. He gasped and steadied himself, pushing back to his feet and wiping his urine-soaked hands on his robes. He grabbed the phone and pulled up a number in the contacts, filed under Building Supplies, and dialed, praying he could convince the man he hadn't cooperated at all.

Kane climbed into their SUV and started the engine as Mo closed the passenger side door. "Did you plant the bugs?"

Mo nodded. "Yeah, I put the listener behind the table he was charging his phone on, and luckily I found the right battery in your satchel." He patted it, still sitting on his lap. "You've got quite the selection in here."

Kane grinned. "Who knew being a Boy Scout would pay off in my line of work."

Mo's eyes narrowed but Kane silenced any question with a wave, instead pressing a combination of buttons on the vehicle's radio. A static-laden transmission began with a bang, then a yelp, then some cursing. He glanced at Mo who shrugged but remained silent as Kane pulled out his laptop, making sure the transmission was being recorded and relayed to Langley. There was a clattering sound, then a phone dialed.

Kane switched the audio over to the phone tap so they could hear both sides of the conversation. He checked the laptop, the number that had been dialed displayed. He sent a quick message to Langley, indicating for them to trace the phone and run voice recognition against the call. If they were lucky, Echelon might have monitored other calls made from this number that could lead them somewhere useful.

The call was finally answered. "Hello?"

"Hi, this is Firash."

"Who?"

"Firash from Cheyabi. We had some dealings last month."

There was a pause. "How did you get this number? I told you we would never see each other again unless you betrayed me."

Kane smiled. This was definitely the coordinator on the ground.

"Forget that," said Firash. "The Americans were just here."

Another pause. "What do you mean by Americans?"

"An American and his translator were just here. They lied to me about selling me something that would cover all my repair costs for what I bought, and then when I let them inside, they attacked me immediately, tied me to a chair, and kept beating on me."

Kane and Mo exchanged bemused glances.

"I didn't tell them anything, I swear, but I think they know who you are. They showed me a photo of you!"

Kane chuckled. This guy was good, slickly laying down a line of bullshit that just might cover his ass.

"And what did you say?"

"I said nothing! I said I didn't recognize you! I'm not a fool! But when they were leaving, the American said he would make it known that I *did* cooperate. But I didn't, I swear!"

"You *are* a fool. I told you when you were paid to tell no one about this, to forget it ever happened. Yet not only did you keep my phone number, you've now called it. Stay where you are. Someone will be there tonight to discuss what happens next."

"I understand."

The call ended and Kane switched the audio over to the bug Mo had planted behind the table. Firash was muttering incoherently, then finally exclaimed, "The new truck!"

Kane glanced over at one of the most unreliable motor vehicles on the road while footfalls faded and grew louder as Firash rushed around his home.

"What do you think he's doing?" asked Mo.

"I think he's packing."

Mo indicated the cursed SUV. "And he thinks he's going to get away in that?"

"He said 'truck.' He might not know better, but I think he's talking about the mosque's truck that he bought. It's probably in good working order."

"What are you going to do? Let him go or take him in?"

The door flew open and Firash burst through carrying several bags. Kane rolled down his window and drew his Glock. He put two in the man's chest then stepped out, straddling the gasping Firash, pointing his weapon directly at the man's forehead.

"This is for killing six Americans who did nothing but try to help you." He fired twice more, delivering the first of what he hoped would be many more sentences over the coming days.

Operations Center 2, CIA Headquarters

Langley, Virginia

Morrison watched as Kane executed one of those involved in massacring American troops. He pointed at the screen. "I clearly saw him reaching for something. Could have been a gun in one of the bags."

Leroux agreed. "Or a bomb."

Tong caught on as Morrison suspected a woman of her talents would. "Special Agent Kane had no choice. He had to shoot him."

Morrison smacked his hands together. "Good. Then we're all in agreement. He followed his ROEs." He turned to Leroux. "What now?"

"We may have just received a treasure trove of intel. We've got a photo of the man, his voice, and his phone number. The fact that it still works almost two months later tells us he's been using the same number the entire time. We should be able to hopefully find intercepts from Echelon and other sources."

"Where is he now?" asked Morrison.

Tong checked. "The call came through a cell tower in Kabul."

"Can we send in a team to pick him up?" asked Child.

Leroux shook his head. "He's long gone. The moment he ended that call, he destroyed the phone and left. We'll still send a team in, though. There might be some residual intel we can use, but we won't be getting him."

Morrison slapped him on the back then headed for the door. "Get to work, people. We don't want to lose this guy. Not when we're so close to finally getting some answers."

Kabul Star Hotel
Kabul, Afghanistan

Abu Mohammed Akhtar ended the call then cursed repeatedly at the stupidity of the man he had just spoken to. He swiped his thumb and deactivated the cellular connection before attaching the phone to his laptop. He launched a program provided by a trusted friend that pulled all the information off the phone then wiped it for when he was switching to a new phone. As the program ran, he rushed into the bathroom, relieved himself, then grabbed his few toiletries and tossed them in his small suitcase. He packed his few belongings, checked that the data transfer on the phone had been completed, then waited impatiently for the wipe to finish. It finally did and he flipped shut his laptop, adding it to the suitcase. He zipped it up, grabbed the phone, then pressed it against the edge of the table and pushed hard, snapping it at the center, rendering it useless.

He grabbed his bag and headed for the door of the modest hotel he had been using as his base of operations for the past two months, each month pre-paid in cash, meaning there was no need to settle a bill. Within five minutes of having ended the call, he was out in the late afternoon sun. He hailed a cab and instructed the driver to head for the nearby bazaar, a crowded place where he could easily lose himself until he procured a new phone and contacted the man he had been dealing with for instructions. He had a mission in two days, and everything had already been arranged. Another American team was due to be targeted, and he didn't want this screwed up because of some idiot.

He didn't know who he was working for. He was certain they weren't Afghan, but the man's Pashto was perfect, though there was a hint of an accent. When contacted several months ago, it had been quite a shock. Two men had shown up at his door, intimidating, with bulging chests indicating shoulder holsters. They were dressed in business suits, something not common in his neighborhood.

He had been leading a quiet life with his family, lost among the masses of his country's biggest city, praying no one ever found out who he actually was. He had once been Al-Qaeda. A personal friend of Bin Laden's. But there had been a falling out. He had objected to the September 11th attack plan. He thought it was too ambitious and feared the wrath it would bring down upon them should it be successful. And he had been right, though had never been given the opportunity to gloat, for he had been forced out for questioning the leadership. Now he was a wanted man, not only by the Americans and their allies, but the Afghan government. He had been on their list for over two decades.

But it was those he called friends, what remained of Al-Qaeda, and of course the Taliban, that he truly feared. They had been after him for years, many assuming he had betrayed the leadership since so many of them were now dead. He had done no such thing, of course. He was loyal to the cause, and if he hadn't been wanted by his own people, he would have joined ISIS and sought a martyr's death. But the only option left to him now was his own personal jihad carried out in silence.

That was until the two men appeared at his door.

"Are you Abu Mohammed Akhtar?"

"No." He immediately closed the door when a foot blocked it open. A suit jacket was drawn aside, a handgun revealed, and the two men "invited" themselves inside. The door was shut and they stepped into the living area. His wife and children could see the fear on his face, and it added to their own. "Everyone into the bedroom." His wife led the children away, all sons, all at the age where they would soon be ready to fight.

The two men sat, indicating for him to do so across from them. "We have a proposition for you, if you are indeed Akhtar."

Akhtar wasn't sure if he should confirm it, though the fact the men were here meant they were already certain. This was a game being played, where what one knew was doled out slowly, as needed, to keep the opponent off guard, to keep them more honest than they were perhaps inclined to be. "If I were, what proposition would you be offering?"

"A way to get back into the fight."

His heart raced with excitement. He was tired of sitting at home while his former friends raged jihad on the infidel invaders, all because he was accused of something he hadn't done. He wanted back in the fight desperately. To die an old man in bed, surrounded by his loved ones, had never been the future he wanted. He wanted to die in glorious battle, taking Americans and Jews with him. "Just what did you have in mind?"

"What is your opinion of the Americans?"

"It hasn't changed, if that's what you're asking."

"Good. And your thoughts on them leaving?"

"The sooner, the better. The sooner the invaders are out, the sooner we can take our country back."

"And you think that's good?"

The question surprised him. "Don't you?"

"If the Americans leave, then how are you going to kill them?"

Akhtar's eyes narrowed at the question, something that had never occurred to him. For as long as he was alive, all he could remember was wanting the outsiders, the invaders, out of his country. He had grown up in the age where the Soviet Union was defeated, then in the aftermath, the Taliban had taken over most of the country, many of them the former Mujahideen supplied by the American government. He and others like him had hoped to create a state where no one else would dare invade, and when Al-Qaeda was seeking a place to train,

Afghanistan was perfect for it. The Americans occasionally hit the country when the terrorist group successfully carried out an attack, but it seldom affected the Afghan people because troops were rarely involved.

He had joined Al-Qaeda as a teenager, and his devotion to the cause had him surging through the ranks. Until they overreached. Using loaded passenger airplanes as flying bombs was brilliant, but it also guaranteed a response like no other. If they had succeeded completely that day, and not only taken out the Twin Towers and part of the Pentagon, but the White House as well, the response might have been far worse than it was. But twenty years later, the original Al-Qaeda was broken, and the only reason the Taliban were resurging was because the Americans were leaving. He couldn't see a reason to keep them here, which brought him back to the curious question.

How would they kill Americans if they were gone?

He shrugged. "We managed before."

"This is true, yes," replied the man. "And look what it got you. Twenty years of occupation."

Akhtar eyed him, the phrasing suggesting the man wasn't Afghan. "What are you getting at?"

"We have a proposal that may extend the American presence in your country, and at the very least will send a message as they depart."

"A very bloody message," said the other, the first time he had spoken. His Pashto had a much thicker accent.

The idea of keeping the Americans here just so that he could kill them wasn't appealing. Too many Western ideas were running amok.

149

He wanted all Westerners and everything they had brought here gone. He had little doubt the central government NATO was leaving behind would swiftly fall, and he would join the jubilant crowds on the streets on that day.

It was the notion of sending a message to the Americans on their way out that intrigued him. "And just what would this message be?"

"We want you to coordinate a series of ambushes on American troops all across the country. You'll use your local knowledge to find volunteers for the attacks that will be paid very handsomely. And for each successful attack, you too will be paid more money than you could possibly imagine."

Akhtar's head slowly bobbed. The money didn't interest him from a personal standpoint, though he of course would use some of it to improve life for his family. But funding for the cause, especially significant funding, might be a way to buy his way back into the good graces of those who would have him dead. And even if it didn't, it meant participating in the death of potentially countless infidels, for the man was right. Once they were out of this country, the likelihood of him having any chance of earning his martyrdom was slim to none.

A deal had been struck.

And for over two months, he had coordinated over half a dozen successful attacks, with several more in the works, including one in two days. He didn't get to participate in the killings directly, but he reveled in the photos, the proof demanded by his partners that the bounty had been earned.

But now there was a chance the Americans had caught up to him.

He should have been more careful. He should have been swapping out his phone more regularly, but it had never occurred to him. He'd hand over a preprogrammed phone, show them how to use it, then collect it when the job was done. He was dealing with simple villagers, most of whom didn't know how to use a cellphone. And now his short-sightedness might have compromised the operation. If the Americans had indeed been there, they might have traced the call and perhaps even recorded it.

But if they had a photo of him, perhaps they had been on to him for some time. Even if that were the case, the phone call he had just received revealed his location. He steadied his hammering heart and reassessed the situation as the taxi approached the bazaar. The Americans didn't know where he was. They might have tracked the phone call back to his hotel room, though he doubted they had that level of accuracy. Even if they could, he wasn't there anymore. And it was no longer a matter of hiding his identity if they had his picture.

It was hiding his location.

That was simple enough, though he'd be more cautious. The question now was what to do? His initial flight was to not only escape the Americans, but to reach out to his contacts to inform them of what had happened, to seek their advice and perhaps their protection. Yet now he was wondering if that was the wisest move. If they found out what had happened, they might cut their ties with him, and he couldn't allow that.

He hadn't felt this alive in years. He was personally responsible for the death of over 30 of the infidels that had invaded his country, and he had no intention of stopping. He had even made contingencies should his contact lose interest. He was saving the money he was getting paid, which was $10,000 per American head. Whoever his partners were, they were overpaying. They could easily find volunteers at half that price, perhaps even a quarter. Should things come to an end with them, he would put together a team himself and keep up their good work for as long as a single American soldier remained on Afghan territory.

When this had all begun, he was torn between whether he wanted the Americans to stay as a result of what he was doing, or to leave. And while he enjoyed participating in the killing and felt it was richly deserved, he would rather have his country free of the infidels and their influence.

And he was determined to make their sendoff as bloody as possible.

That brought him back to what he should do. If the roles were reversed and his partners told him they had been compromised, he would cut all ties. It was just the proper thing to do. It was how things in Al-Qaeda had worked. Few knew anything beyond what their cell needed to know, so if anyone were caught, the damage was compartmentalized. And he had been compromised. He should be cut loose, so that the mission could continue.

He stared out the window, disgusted by the number of unaccompanied women wearing revealing clothing. He had to continue the fight to rid his country of these invaders as quickly as possible, then turn his attention to the central government. They were doomed. They didn't have the heart. Once the Taliban attacked in force, they would scatter to the wind. The country would be back under Taliban control in short order, and Muslims of good faith would yet again have a place to flock to and eventually, one day, help establish the Worldwide Caliphate. He breathed deeply, his chest swelling, and he smiled with the knowledge that in the end, Allah would triumph over the Western evil.

And his decision was made.

He would acquire a new phone, inform his partners that he was switching as a precaution, then find a new hotel to hole up in. And if it proved the wrong decision, then so be it. He would take down as many of those who came for him as he could before dying a martyr in the jihad against the infidels.

Then he would enjoy his reward in Jannah for eternity.

A prospect that brought a broader smile.

Cheyabi, Afghanistan

Kane searched the body, relieving it of the satellite phone. He continued when someone yelled behind him in Pashto.

"Hey, what's going on here?"

A woman screamed and Kane spun to see a group of people walking toward him, including women and children. He ignored them and instead climbed into the SUV, closing the door. More shouts erupted as he started the engine and Mo fastened his seatbelt.

"I wasn't expecting you to shoot him."

Kane put the vehicle in gear and glanced at the man he considered a friend. "Really? I never thought I wouldn't." He disabled the traction control and hammered on the gas as he spun the wheel, sending up a dust cloud as more people emerged from their homes.

"AK-47 to our right."

Kane straightened out as he accelerated toward the road that would take them back to the airport. Gunfire rang out behind them, the distinctive ping of bullets ricocheting off the reinforced vehicle causing Mo to duck and Jafar, bound in the back seat, to scream against his gag. Kane, however, remained calm as he kept one eye on the road ahead and the other on the rear-view mirror where he could see the gunman, already having lost control of his weapon, his inexperience coupled with the full-automatic setting sending the barrel kicking up and to the right, firing uselessly into the air.

Kane pressed harder on the accelerator, putting more distance between them and the danger, and in less than a minute, they were outside of the main village. He eased off the gas, the roads in such piss-poor shape they weren't meant for high-speed travel.

"We should be safe now." He jerked a thumb over his shoulder. "Why don't you untie our friend before he ends up shitting himself."

Mo removed his seatbelt then turned around. He removed the gag and cut the zip ties binding Jafar's hands and feet.

"You just murdered that man!" cried Jafar, pressing into the corner, putting as much distance between him and Kane as he could in the confined space. "Why would you do that? What did he ever do to you?"

"Take the wheel."

Mo's hand darted out, gripping the wheel as Kane turned and delivered a punch to Jafar's nose. Nothing too hard, just something to get the man's attention. "He did what you did. He took the money. He helped kill six American soldiers, just like you did. He deserved to die, just like you do. There's only one difference between you and him. He kept the money for himself, but you gave it to your village. That's the only reason you're alive right now, so keep your mouth shut, answer any questions I have when I ask them, and when I'm finished with you, I'll decide what I'm doing with you."

Jafar's eyes were saucers as he shrunk even deeper into his corner. Kane turned back to face the road, taking the wheel from Mo, and steadied his rage. He had just killed a man, a man he had always intended to kill, for the bastard had one motivation—greed. Jafar was alive because he needed him for information, but also his motivation appeared to at least be driven by helping his community. It in no way excused what he did, and the man would likely be dead before the day was out, for Kane wasn't convinced he was useful anymore. He had taken him initially as a human shield and because he was the only one who had seen the contact that was at least a middleman in this entire conspiracy.

But now they had a photo of the man in question.

He frowned. Or did they? He glanced at Mo. "Show him the photo."

Mo pulled out the tablet and brought up the photo they had taken off the dead man's phone. He showed it to Jafar, whose eyes grew wide as his head rapidly bobbed. "Yes, that's him! That's the man who paid me!"

Unfortunately for Jafar, his excitement was misplaced, as he had just put another nail in his coffin, any use he had now gone. Kane pulled out the comms from the center console and jacked in. "Control, this is Diggler. Come in, over."

Leroux answered immediately. "This is Control. Go ahead, Diggler."

"We're sending you that photo now. It's been confirmed by two of those involved that this is their contact who arranged the attacks and paid them their money." He gestured to Mo to transmit the photo. Mo tapped on the tablet several times and gave a nod. "It should be coming in now. That face and the voice you got in that recording from the phone call should be the same person. Run them against every database you've got. I have a feeling that with how well these operations have been coordinated, this is somebody with experience. He might be in our files."

"Roger that, Diggler. We're already running the voice and the phone number that was called. We've got the photo now. We'll get on it. What are you going to do with your witness?"

Kane glanced in the rearview mirror, Jafar sitting there, ignorant to what they were talking about. "I think he's outlived his usefulness."

"Agreed. The Chief just relayed new orders from the President. All those we can confirm involved are now on the Termination List."

"Understood. I'll contact you when we reach the airport. Diggler, out."

Kane returned his focus to his driving, saying nothing as he contemplated the situation. He wouldn't kill Jafar yet, but unless he could think of a reason to keep him alive, the man wouldn't be boarding the plane. He was of slightly mixed feelings about it. He had no qualms about killing in the heat of battle or through more covert means, like a sniper rifle, a bomb, poison, or any other number of methods he had employed over the years. But double-tapping someone a few feet from his face who was otherwise likely a good person who merely lived by a different set of values, did give him pause, though only for a moment.

This was a man who had been offered money to murder innocent people and had taken it. It didn't matter that he gave it to the village to improve the lives of those he held dear. It was still murder. Those in Afghanistan might live under a different moral compass than back home, but that didn't matter.

Some moral compasses were wrong.

He sighed, and Mo picked up on it.

"What's wrong?"

"I have to kill him."

"Is that necessary?"

"Orders. Anyone involved is to be eliminated. I guess Washington wants a message sent."

Mo's head bobbed. "I can see that. When do you plan on doing it?"

He sighed again. "I was going to wait, but I guess sooner is better. Put him out of his misery."

"What if he has more intel?"

Kane shook his head. "That photo and the phone number I'm betting are going to crack this wide open. This guy is a patsy in this."

"Does he deserve to die for just being a patsy?"

"He was still a willing participant. It's not like he was framed and is actually an innocent man."

"You mean innocent like Oswald?"

Kane gave Mo a look. "Have you been watching JFK again?"

Mo shrugged. "I admit nothing."

Kane laughed and Jafar's curious puppy dog look had him coming to a decision. He removed his foot from the accelerator and gently pressed the brakes, bringing them to a halt on the side of the road. He climbed out then opened the rear door. "Let's go," he said in Pashto.

Jafar stared at him wide-eyed. "Why? What's happening?"

Kane removed his weapon and flicked it at Jafar. "Get out, now."

Jafar's eyes welled with tears as he scrambled from the SUV. "Please don't kill me. I can help you. I'll do whatever I have to do to make up for what I did."

Kane ignored the pleas. He had heard them scores of times in his career from people responsible for far less than what this man had done. Kane stepped back in case the man attempted something stupid, and noted that Mo was looking away, not wanting to see what was about to happen. It was one of the uglier parts of his job, but at least 30 good American soldiers were dead along with their translators because men like this had said yes.

An engine roared and Kane spun. A box van he recognized as the new one purchased for the mosque in the village they had just left careened around the bend. He cursed at the sight of an AK-47 hanging out the passenger side window, the muzzle flashes reaching him before the reports of the shots.

"Get down!" he shouted, for Mo's sake, not Jafar's.

He hit the dirt, rolling under the SUV as he extended his weapon toward the oncoming threat. Jafar cried out in terror but Kane ignored him, instead taking a bead on the engine block of the approaching vehicle. He emptied a mag into the belly of the beast and quickly reloaded, emptying two more.

"Ammo!" he yelled. "Center console!"

"Just a second!" replied Mo, his voice trembling.

Two mags dropped in the dirt beside the open driver's side door. Kane reached out and grabbed them, reloading as the vehicle hissed to a halt, not 20 yards from their position. He rolled out from under his cover and took a knee, removing the man with the gun from the equation. The other three in the cab of the truck jumped out and ran back toward their village, and he let them be. They might very well have been involved in the ambush, but they could just as easily be members of the family of the man he had executed, seeking revenge.

He turned and frowned. Jafar was down, blood staining his robes, at least three rounds taken to the chest by the high-powered weapon. Kane took a knee and checked for a pulse, finding none, and was relieved he hadn't been the one to deliver the fatal rounds. He closed the man's eyes, still wide with the horror of his final moments, but successfully suppressed any urge to say a prayer on the man's behalf.

No one had been there to pray for his victims.

Kane climbed back inside and closed the door. Mo pushed himself up into his seat, peering out the windows of the other side.

"Jafar?"

"Dead."

"Did you…"

Kane shook his head. "No, friendly fire I suppose is one way to look at it. Either way, the job's done. He's paid for his crimes." He put the vehicle back in gear and pulled away from the side of the road, putting some distance between them and the village, just in case another posse was assembled. They had a long drive ahead of them, and if there was more than one satellite phone in that village, they could never outrun a space-based communications system.

He just hoped they boarded that airplane before anyone could coordinate a real response.

Pul-e Khishti Bazaar
Kabul, Afghanistan

Akhtar smiled as the newly-activated phone rang in his hand, the vendor confirming it was in working order by placing a call. Money exchanged hands and Akhtar strode casually away, heading back to his hotel and new base of operations. It had been several hours, and he was still alive, which meant nobody had caught him on camera, or if they had, they had lost him in the crowded market as he had expected.

With his new phone in hand, he dialed his contact. It rang several times before someone finally answered, obviously hesitant at the new number. "Hello?"

"This is Akhtar. I just wanted you to know I have a new number."

There was a pause. "Why?"

He had prepared himself for the question. "I just thought it was wise to switch phones. I'm going to do it after each operation from now on. It's better for security."

"After two months, you decide it's necessary now? What's happened?"

Akhtar tensed. "Nothing, I swear. I just thought it was a good idea."

"It's been my experience that those telling the truth don't have to swear upon anything. Now, I'll give you one final chance to tell the truth, or I'm hanging up and you'll never hear from us again."

Akhtar closed his eyes, his shoulders slumping in defeat. Everything was slipping away. "One of the local contacts pulled my phone number from the cellphone I gave him. He just called me and told me that the Americans had paid him a visit."

"What else?"

"Nothing, I…" He caught himself. "I promise you." It was a lie, of course, having omitted the fact the Americans had his photo.

For a moment, there was silence on the other end of the line. "Where are you now?"

"I'm in a new location. I'm secure."

"If the Americans have your photo, you're anything but secure. Give me your exact location. We're going to send a team in to collect you and your family until we can be sure how bad the security breach is."

Akhtar hesitated. There could be no doubt about the security breach and that he was now compromised. The order to have him stay put and wait to be collected along with his family was reminiscent of the old days in Al-Qaeda. When something went wrong, they would send in a cleanup crew and eliminate the problem.

Had he just become a problem?

"Is there a problem?" asked the man at his lack of response.

Akhtar gulped. "Not at all." He gave him the address of the hotel he was at.

"Stay where you are. Somebody will come get you within a few hours."

"And my family?"

"They'll be collected as well, then you'll be reunited. Understood?"

"Yes."

The call disconnected and he sat shaking on his bed. He had always thought that death didn't scare him, but now that he knew without a doubt he'd be dead before the day was out, the prospect terrified him, despite the knowledge he would die a martyr to the cause and receive his promised reward in Jannah. He drew a deep breath, holding it for a moment as he steadied his nerves. As he slowly calmed, he weighed his options. He could stay here and gamble that they didn't intend to kill him, he could leave and go into hiding, or he could leave and attempt to save his family and go into hiding together.

He rose and paced the length of the small room, scratching at his thick beard. He wasn't staying here and waiting for death. That was a coward's way out. His obligation was to save his family. He had plenty of money set aside from these operations that could be used to get them out of the country. But if he were to save his family, he'd have to act quickly.

He grabbed his bag, still packed, and headed out the door, wishing he had permitted his wife a cellphone of her own. Unfortunately, no one in the household had a phone, and his mistrust of his own family could prove the death of them.

Operations Center 2, CIA Headquarters

Langley, Virginia

"His name is Abu Mohammed Akhtar, a former Al-Qaeda lieutenant, close to Bin Laden," explained Leroux to Morrison, who folded his arms and scratched his chin as he stared at the file photos on the main displays.

"So, Al-Qaeda is behind this?"

Leroux shook his head. "I wouldn't be so sure of that. Apparently, there was a falling out between him and the leadership around the time of Nine-Eleven. From what we can gather, he disagreed with the attacks."

Morrison's eyebrows shot up and he turned to Leroux. "He disagreed? That was their greatest victory ever."

"He felt it would bring too harsh a response."

Child grunted. "He was right about that."

"He was forced out just around the same time we gained some traction after catching a few of his comrades. We were able to make a string of arrests, kill off quite a few of their leadership, and because of the timing, the Al-Qaeda brass assumed he had betrayed them out of revenge. They want him as much as we want him."

Morrison chewed his cheek. "Reconciliation?"

Leroux shrugged. "It's always possible."

"The enemy of my enemy is my friend," muttered Tong.

Leroux agreed. "Exactly."

Morrison glanced at Tong. "Bravo Team is already inbound. We'll have boots on the ground in Kabul in the morning to act on any intel you gather."

"Don't we already have teams there?" asked Child. "We've been fighting there for twenty years."

Morrison turned slightly to face the youngest member of the team who still hadn't figured out that brain-to-mouth filter. "Yes, we have Special Forces there, however, you might be surprised to learn that with the pullout, they're all tasked with other duties. Bravo Team will only have one job." He returned his attention to Leroux. "To be perfectly honest, I didn't think you'd get us a target so quickly otherwise I would have had them sent sooner."

Leroux shrugged. "You only have yourself to blame, sir. You should know my team is the best."

Child shoved two hands in the air as he spun in his chair. "Hell yeah!"

Morrison shook his head at the display, though a slight smirk appeared as he headed for the door. "Keep up the good work, people."

Leroux cleared his throat. "Umm, sir?"

Morrison turned and stopped. "What?"

"I was just informed by Fort Meade that our priority request for Echelon has been denied. Apparently, something big is going on there. They need an authorization, director level or above, to prioritize our request."

Morrison pulled out his phone. "Consider it done." He resumed his departure as someone he was on a first-name basis with answered his call. "Hey, Theresa, I understand you need an authorization from me." The door hissed closed behind the Chief and a moment later a message came in on Leroux's workstation. He sat at his chair and brought it up.

Priority authorization received.

He smiled as the noose around Akhtar grew a little tighter.

Outside Akhtar Residence

Kabul, Afghanistan

Akhtar stood just down the street from his home, peering at the front gate. He had arrived about ten minutes ago, remaining in the shadows, his face covered and one leg held tucked up under his robes by a tied scarf. He leaned on a cane, feigning an amputation, as he watched every single person that came and went, listened to every sound, every word carried on the gentle breeze. And found nothing suggesting anyone was waiting for him.

American or otherwise.

He couldn't delay any longer. It had been nearly an hour since his phone call with his contact, and longer since the one with the moron. They could be here any minute. He hobbled across the street, maintaining the pretense of an amputee, and was soon at the front gate. He turned the handle and pushed it open, frowning at the fact it had been left unlocked, contrary to the instructions he had given his wife.

She would be taught a lesson about listening to her husband when this was over. He pushed the gate aside and stepped in, reaching down and yanking at the knot on the scarf before easing his cramped leg to the ground. He closed the gate then crossed the courtyard and entered the house the stone walls hid from prying eyes. He shook his head once again at it being unlocked as he closed the door.

"It's me! Everybody come here at once!"

Nobody replied.

"Is anyone here?" His heart pounded as he moved deeper into the house, though his oncoming panic might be misplaced. They could be at the market. It was possible his wife needed something, and of course, she would require an escort of a male relative. Their oldest would fit that bill, and the rest would have come out of boredom or duty to protect their mother. It might also explain why everything was unlocked, his family perhaps feeling security wasn't necessary if they weren't there. There was nothing here worth stealing.

He passed the kitchen and turned the corner then cried out, collapsing to his knees at the sight of his wife huddled over their youngest, shielding him as his eldest three did the same for their mother, all to no avail, their bullet-ridden bodies unmoving, frozen in their final moments on Allah's creation.

He had taken too long to get here. He never should have called his partners. Not before securing his family. There was no doubt they were cleaning up the operation, murdering his family in case he had told them anything, and now they would be eliminating him should they find him. He pushed to his feet, rage mixing with the sorrow and anguish. He now had a new enemy, an enemy who had to pay for this atrocity, for indiscriminately killing the innocent.

Yet how he could find them, he had no idea.

He sniffed hard then did something that could prove fatal. He pulled out his phone and dialed the number for his contact. It was answered immediately.

"I thought I told you to wait."

"And I thought you said you were collecting my family."

"What are you talking about?"

"My wife and sons are dead. Don't pretend you don't know what happened."

"I *don't* know what happened. Our team hasn't arrived there yet. They should be there in the next few minutes. Stay where you are. We'll come get you and bring you to safety."

"If you didn't do this, then who did?"

"It had to be the Americans. They must have somehow found out where your family lived. Now stay where you are. We'll be there soon."

The call ended and he stood frozen, staring at the bodies of his family, debating what to do. A moment ago, he had been convinced that his partners had killed his family, but now he wasn't so sure. Could it have been the Americans? It wouldn't surprise him. The infidels were the tools of the Devil and had no respect for the lives of the innocent.

Yet how had they found him? The phone that had been compromised was new, purchased after he had set himself up in the hotel months ago. It had never been used in his home, and he had never called here, as there were no phones to call. How had they found this place, even if they had traced all of his calls, listened to everything he had said?

He had sent money to his family through friends, yet still, there should be no way to trace his family through them. If the Americans already had his photo, how long had they been working on this? He shook his head. The only people who always knew this location were his partners. They had shown up at his house to make the offer. And what was more likely? That they had come here and killed his family, cleaning up loose ends just like he used to in the old days, or that the Americans had somehow found his family and slaughtered them?

As much as he hated the Americans, as much as he wanted every single one of them dead, this wasn't the way they worked. They would have arrested his family and used them as leverage to get him to turn himself in, with the local Afghan forces used as proxies.

The front gate creaked, snapping him back to reality. He shoved the table in the center of the room aside then flipped over a rug crafted by his great-grandmother so many decades ago and proudly maintained by his wife, whose blood now stained it. A hole was revealed, covered by a sheet of plywood. He flipped it up and reached inside, grabbing an AK-47 and several magazines. He stuffed them in his pockets along with two grenades.

Whoever was coming through the door was going to die. He no longer cared. If the Americans were here to arrest him, he would have fought them to the death regardless. But if it were his partners, whom he was once again convinced had murdered his family, then they too deserved to die, even if they were fellow Muslims.

He pulled the pin from one of the grenades then gripped it tight in his hand as he flipped the AK-47 on its side, resting it on the edge of the turned-over table, aiming it toward the hallway that led to the door. Whoever it was knocked, and it gave him pause. Would men sent to kill, knock first? The door opened and his pulse pounded in his ears as he waited for what was to come, uncertain if he were about to greet friend or foe. He could hear the footfalls of several people, whispering instructions to each other in a language he recognized.

And his eyes shot wide as he realized he hadn't been serving his cause at all.

He had been serving that of his enemy.

He roared in rage as the first appeared. He threw his grenade into the hallway then gripped his AK-47 tight as he squeezed the trigger, fulfilling his dream of dying as a martyr. "Allahu Akbar!" he repeatedly shouted as lead pumped from the weapon. The first man dropped before a shot could be fired in response as three more men surged into the room, their assault rifles spewing as they escaped the grenade, Akhtar having made the critical mistake of not counting off before throwing it.

His weapon fell silent and he cursed as he ejected the empty magazine. As he fumbled to reload, a long-practiced move now forgotten, the men broke to the side as the grenade exploded. The massive detonation in the confined space was overwhelming, shrapnel and flames erupting into the living area, taking one of the men down.

But only one.

The other two opened fire as he squeezed the trigger, and as each of their rounds found its mark, Akhtar continued to cry out, "Allahu Akbar!" as he silently prayed he would still be granted access to Jannah, a paradise he had fought so hard for, despite the fact he had been used, and was merely a tool of those he wanted dead.

Approaching Kunduz, Afghanistan

Kane checked the nav system. They were fifteen minutes from the airstrip, and their flight was due to leave in thirty. The turnaround time from past experience suggested the plane might already be on the ground. So far, there had been no further attempts to intercept them, however there were no communities between the attempted assault and the airport.

The road to the airport would be the first opportunity.

If word had been sent ahead, this was where they would be ambushed. Mo had scrambled into the back seat earlier and folded them down, giving him access to the secure lockup in the back. Both of them now had not only handguns and extra ammo, but body armor and an M4 should things get hairy.

His comms squawked in his ear. "Diggler, Control. We've got activity ahead, over."

"Copy that, Control. What are we looking at?"

"We're showing a vehicle waiting by the side of the road about two klicks ahead, and another one two klicks beyond that. It could be nothing, but I just thought you should be aware."

"Copy that, Control. Have you been able to reach our pilot?"

"Affirmative. He says he's fueled and ready to go the moment you arrive if there's any trouble."

"Copy that, Control. Tell him if he doesn't fly off like a coward, beers are on me, and Mo will give him a big sloppy kiss."

Mo's eyes shot wide at the one side of the conversation he could hear as Leroux chuckled at the other end. "I'm sure that's incentive enough to keep any man on the ground under gunfire." Leroux's tone changed. "Diggler, you should see the first vehicle coming up on your right."

Kane spotted the pick-up truck that had seen better days, the burning oil wisping from its tailpipe indicating it was idling. Two men sat in the cab, the driver staring in his mirror, watching as they approached.

Yet it still could be nothing.

"Stand by, Control." He glanced at Mo, his Glock gripped tightly in his lap, his finger on the trigger. "Trigger discipline, my friend."

Mo flinched. "Huh?"

"Get your finger off the trigger. Unless you're going to shoot that thing, keep it on the guard."

Mo shook out a nod, adjusting his finger position so he didn't blow his own kneecap off if startled.

176

"First sign of trouble, duck. The metal in that door will protect you far more than that glass. Remember, it's bullet-resistant, not bullet-proof. We're just going to…" He cursed as two men that had been lying flat in the back of the truck sat up, AK-47s in their hands, lead belching at them within moments. "Control, Diggler. We're taking fire. Repeat, we're taking fire." He hammered on the gas as the bullets pinged off the up-armored SUV. They blasted past the vehicle and he glanced in his rearview mirror as a cloud of dust indicated the beginning of their pursuit. "You okay?" he asked Mo.

"I think so, though I may have to change my undergarments."

Kane laughed, remaining calm as the gunfire continued ineffectually behind them—it was far more challenging to aim standing in the back of a pickup truck on a rough road.

"Diggler, the next vehicle is just ahead. They're pulling onto the road to block you."

Kane watched as another pickup truck came to a halt, blocking the road. The driver stepped out as Kane lowered the window, extending his Glock and steadying his hand on the side mirror. He opened fire, taking out the driver with his first two shots, then adjusted his aim slightly as he eliminated one of the two men in the back, sending the other scurrying for cover.

Shooting from a vehicle at high speeds was something he trained for. His little game with Fang a few days ago wasn't just for fun. Zombie Paintball Racing, as she had called it, required incredible skill to do properly, and as long as the zombie element remained out of this, he should be okay.

His balls sent him an aching reminder of why that was so important.

"Best path forward?"

"It's wide enough on the left," replied Leroux.

"Copy that." He didn't take his foot off the accelerator. Instead, he kept them aimed at the truck before pulling his arm inside and dropping his weapon in his lap before taking the wheel with both hands. He jerked them to the left, passing between the front bumper of the driverless vehicle and a set of large rocks on the side of the road. He steered back onto the pavement and checked his rearview mirror to see the second vehicle coming to a halt, blocked by the first. More shots were fired in their general direction, but they were out of range. "Control, Diggler. Anything else we should know about on our route ahead?"

"Not at this time, Diggler. We'll send the drone ahead to recheck. Stand by."

Kane glanced over at Mo, somehow wedged in the footwell. "How in the hell did you fit in there?"

"I am a very small man. Sometimes it has advantages."

Kane laughed. "Well, you're safe now, so you can sit up."

"Are you sure? They're still shooting at us."

"Buddy, they're way out of range. Don't worry."

Mo struggled back into his seat. "Who do you think they were?" he finally asked, his voice still quivering.

"There's not a lot of possibilities. They were clearly waiting for us, so it's definitely connected to the visit we just paid. It's either his friends or family, or the people he's been dealing with."

"Which one do you think it was?"

"I'm guessing friends or family. The chances of Akhtar having people in the area already are slim to none."

"He might have called in some local favors."

Kane shook his head. "No, remember, only the villagers saw our vehicle, and they wouldn't know how to contact Akhtar. I think this was friends and family. There's obviously another satphone in the village. They called ahead, told members of the clan that live in this area what had happened, what our vehicle looked like, and when we had left. This was just a failed attempt to deliver justice for a crime they felt was committed."

"Do you think it's over?"

Kane flashed him a grin. "Not for a second."

Outside Kunduz, Afghanistan

Ben Ledger checked his watch and frowned. He was due to take off in ten minutes, and Kane wasn't here yet. He had dealt with him before, and the man was never early. And was definitely not an insurance investigator. But it wasn't his job to ask those types of questions. His job was to ferry people from one point to another in a country quickly falling apart. It made his job more difficult as each day passed, and with the Taliban resurging, he had been forced to cut out several of his regular routes as they were no longer safe to land at, even if the area surrounding the airport was secure. The Taliban were taking potshots at planes, hoping to get lucky as the flights were on approach. They knew that if they managed to take out an aircraft, they were definitely killing Westerners or government officials, all of whom were prime targets as far as the fundamentalists were concerned.

He had seen enough action in the Australian Special Air Service, his 20-year stint in the military ended in a damn car accident and not on the battlefield. His kids were grown up and moved out, and his wife was shacked up with the doctor who had performed his back surgery after the accident, the divorce papers apparently sitting on his table at home. He'd sign them as soon as he got back, which would be soon. Once the Americans pulled out, this country was going to shit, and he'd be flying his plane somewhere far safer than this hellhole.

But the money was good, damn good, so it was worth the risk to stick around until the end. Especially when it was people like Kane. He had no doubt whoever the man actually worked for was fully aware of exactly who their pilot was, and what he had accomplished in his career, and they were counting on his skills should something go wrong.

He cursed as something went wrong.

Four vehicles raced along the single road that gave access through the easily breachable fence. He turned to his flight attendant and old army buddy, Michael Clarke. "Make sure everything's buttoned down. I think we're going to be leaving here in a hurry."

"Yes, sir."

"And get Ginger ready, but keep her out of sight of the passengers."

"That bad, huh?"

"I don't know. You tell me." Ledger gestured toward the four vehicles, slowing to make the turn through the gate.

Clarke eyed him. "Is there a reason we're sticking around?"

Ledger pursed his lips. There was no point in waiting for Kane if they were dead. "All right. Let's get going." There was also no point in waiting to see what these new arrivals wanted. They either wanted one of his passengers, or they wanted Kane. Neither was good. He rushed up the steps, Clarke on his heels, ignoring the concerned questions from the passengers who had also spotted the vehicles, weapons on full display.

He skipped the pre-flight checklist, instead instinctively flipping and turning every switch and knob that needed to be dealt with. The engines roared to life as Clarke poked his head in the cockpit, closing the door.

"Is Ginger ready?"

Clarke slid aside a hidden panel and pulled out the F88 Austeyr assault rifle, flicking off the safety. "She's ready."

"Then get your ass in that door, and if anybody fires at us, open up on them."

Clarke sighed, shaking his head. "I knew I never should have agreed to come work for you."

Ledger released the brakes as he throttled up, the plane jerking forward. "Ah, you love it and you know it."

"I didn't say I didn't love it. I just said I shouldn't have taken the job." Clarke disappeared, and through the open door, those outside shouting at the plane were drowned out by the protests from the passengers demanding to know what was going on. Clarke delivered an expletive-ridden tirade at them, leaving them in stunned silence, and if

Ledger gave a shit about customer service reviews, he was sure some colorful complaints would be left on Yelp after this flight landed.

A shot rang out as he turned onto the runway, and Ginger responded, Clarke leaving it on single shot so he could pick his targets more carefully and conserve ammo. Ledger had no idea who they were facing. It shouldn't be Taliban, not in this area, but anything was possible these days. He slid the window open on his left and poked his head out. Clarke had taken a few of them down, and the others were cowering behind their vehicles with no sign of any coordinated effort to retaliate. These were amateurs who had little to no battlefield experience.

He completed his turn onto the runway and shoved the throttle to full. "Button us up!" he shouted, leaving the door open useless now that Clarke was on the wrong side of the aircraft to engage. The cabin noise behind him quieted dramatically, and as he reached takeoff speed, he pulled back on the stick. The nose lifted and moments later they were in the air. He made sure he gained at least 100 feet of altitude then banked away from the airport in case those on the ground decided they wanted to continue firing.

Clarke reappeared, Ginger gripped in his hand. "What the hell was that all about?"

Ledger shrugged. "I'm guessing you screwed up somebody's drink order on the last flight."

Clarke flipped him the bird. "That's why I only offer water."

Ledger gently banked to starboard as he gained altitude. "If I had to hazard a guess, I'd say this is all about them." He pointed down at the road below where a black SUV barreled toward the airport, matching the make and model that Kane had driven away in earlier in the day. He banked hard, lining up with the road, then dropped to the deck, buzzing the SUV. He steered hard to port, staring out the window, and spotted Kane waving. Ledger stuck a hand out the window and pointed at the ground below, then continued to loop around, lining up once again with the road.

Clarke cursed. "You're not going to do what I think you're going to do, are you?"

"That depends. What do you think I'm going to do?"

"Something unbelievably stupid."

Ledger flashed him a grin. "You *do* know me."

Back home in Australia, this wouldn't be a hazardous move—the roads could be expected to be decent. But here, roads were garbage, though this one, at least from his position, didn't appear to be too bad, with signs of recent repairs having been completed. Not surprising, since this was the only road into the airport and the nearby town, and the government wanted people to think progress was being made.

He jerked a thumb over his shoulder. "Better warn them."

Clarke disappeared and Ledger chuckled as his friend shouted in several languages. "Tighten your seatbelts, grab your knees, and be prepared to kiss your asses goodbye. If we survive this, the next round's on me." Clarke reappeared and strapped into the co-pilot seat as Ledger shook his head at him.

"You always know the right thing to say."

Clarke shrugged. "If I hadn't joined the military, I'm sure I would've become a poet."

Ledger roared in laughter as the tires chirped and he steadied their heading on the road. He powered down and raised the flaps, applying the brakes as the speed indicator quickly dropped. They raced past Kane's SUV, parked well off the road to give them room, the aircraft's wingspan wider than the sunbaked asphalt. He came to a halt then turned them around as Kane's SUV skidded to a halt, Kane and his translator immediately exiting, the other Afghan that had been with them nowhere to be seen.

"Let them in."

Clarke was way ahead of him, already out of his seat and moving toward the passenger cabin. Ledger leaned out his window. "Get a wiggle on, would you? Whoever the hell's after you has got a lot of friends waiting for us at the airport."

Kane acknowledged him with a wave and within moments the two men and their luggage were inside and Clarke had the door closed. Kane stepped into the cockpit. "Let's get the hell out of here."

Ledger pushed forward on the throttle. "You don't have to ask me twice." The plane slowly picked up speed, the acceleration gaining as the engines built up power. He pointed at the co-pilot seat. "Do you know how to fly?"

Kane sat, strapping in. "They teach us everything at Insurance School."

Ledger laughed. "I have no doubt. I just didn't know Shaw's of London had a school at Bragg or the Farm."

Kane flashed him a grin. "I have no idea what you're talking about."

Operations Center 2, CIA Headquarters
Langley, Virginia

Child whistled as he stared at his workstation. "I love it when people don't follow proper security protocols."

Leroux turned in his chair to face his underling. "What have you got?"

"I've got Echelon intercepts coming out the yin-yang. It looks like this guy has been using the same phone for almost three months. I can put him in the area of all seven suspected attacks, and if he's following the pattern, there could be more."

"How many more?"

"Three." He tapped at his keyboard. "I just sent you them."

Leroux checked his station then forwarded the information to Tong. "Sonya, have these checked out. See if we've got attacks in the area or attempted attacks. The Chief's going to want to tie everything we can to these people if we're going to do what I suspect

Washington's going to want." He turned back to Child. "What's the pattern?"

"It looks like minimal communication with whoever his contacts are. He gets a call with two or three locations. That's it. Nothing else is said. Then within a few days, he gets a phone call from whatever local contact he's convinced to participate in an attack. From what I've skimmed so far, it appears everyone says yes. They provide a date and time for when our troops will be in their village, then he calls his handlers, gives them the name of the village, the date and time, then hangs up. Then a couple of days after the attack, he gets a phone call from his recruit confirming the attack and asking to meet. Then after the meeting, there's a final phone call to his handler indicating receipt of the photographs and confirmation of how many were killed and that payment was made, then that's it."

"Pretty minimalist," said Tong.

Leroux agreed. "Probably designed to reduce the chance of tracing the calls or of eavesdropping. Considering their success rate, it would appear it was effective. I assume we have the numbers for the incoming and outgoing calls?"

Child nodded. "According to the Echelon analyst, the numbers are being run now, and they should have more for us any minute. Whoever the Chief called dropped the hammer on them, so they're getting everything they can to us as fast as they can."

Leroux smiled slightly. "Good."

Child continued to scan. "I might have an explanation for why three of those locations I sent aren't on our list."

Leroux's eyes narrowed. "What?"

"It looks like for those villages, the people he recruited ultimately turned him down."

"So, there are a few people with morals over there," muttered Tong.

"More than a few, I hope," said Leroux. "If that country stands any chance, the population has to stand up and fight back against those who would take them back down the path of hatred and Dark Ages thinking."

Child clicked his mouse then his eyes swung back and forth over a new message before his jaw dropped. "Holy shit!"

Everyone turned to face him.

"What?" asked Leroux finally after Child remained silent, continuing to read.

"I just got another update from Echelon. The number of his handlers has been traced."

"Who does it belong to?"

Child shrugged. "No idea. It's a burner. But that's not what's important here. It looks like the phone initially came online in Syria."

"Syria?" It had never occurred to Leroux that Syria could be involved. It had enough of its own problems, though it was one piece of good news. Syria was a country they could hit and hit hard without any real threat of reprisals. "I'm going to—"

Child cut him off. "Forget Syria. That's not what's key here."

Leroux leaned forward in anticipation. "What is?"

"It's where the very first call from Syria was made to." The fear on Child's face had Leroux tensing.

"Where?"

Child lowered his voice, as if afraid the wrong people might overhear. "Moscow."

Bagram Airfield-BAF

Bagram, Afghanistan

Kane sat with Mo, sipping on a bottle of ice-cold water as Ledger and his partner slowly circled his plane, searching for any damage. They were at Bagram Airfield, about as secure as you could get in this country, Langley having called off his scouting mission now that the new intel had arrived. Not only was there a possible Syrian link, but Russian as well. And to top it off, the central government authorities had just reported that Akhtar was dead, found shot with his wife and children, along with three other men. Langley was running their faces now. He was guessing a clean-up crew had been sent in to eliminate Akhtar, but the man had fought back. The question was whether they were locals hired to do the job, or part of the team on the ground sent in by the Russians or Syrians.

He personally couldn't believe it was the Syrians. That country was in disarray and could ill afford the wrath of America should it be found out. But Russia was an entirely different matter, and the implications were unthinkable. Several years ago, the Iranians had run a bounty operation where they paid a thousand a head for dead Americans, but that was expected of a regime like that, where its only method of warfare was terror. But for Russia to do something like this was inconceivable.

To pay out massive bounties for the murder of American soldiers was essentially an act of war. The problem was, how do you respond? America certainly had the capability to retaliate. There were any number of hard targets within Russia and its allies, including Syria, that they could hit, but an overt military strike could lead to all-out war.

And that had to be what the Kremlin was thinking, that America wouldn't risk war. Personally, he'd like to drop a MOAB on the Kremlin. The Mother Of All Bombs would level the place and certainly send a message. Unfortunately, the reply would likely be nuclear. No, before they reacted to this intel, they had to know for sure that the Russians were involved, then decide upon how to deliver a message that wouldn't result in war, but would make it clear that if it ever happened again, the consequences would be dire.

Blood had to be drawn.

Mo finished his own bottle of water, then regarded him. "You haven't said much since you got that last transmission."

Kane shook his head. "No, I suppose I haven't."

"Was it bad news?"

"You could say that."

"Anything you can talk about?"

Kane shook his head. "Trust me. You don't want to know."

"That bad?"

"It could be. Once your escort gets here, I want you to go home. Forget about what happened. Enjoy your kid's birthday party, but do something for me."

"What's that?"

"Pack a go-bag for each of your family members, just in case."

Mo gulped. "It's really that bad?"

"Possibly. If anything suspicious happens, anything that raises concern, don't hesitate. Head to any American installation. I've already had your names added to the Local Asset List. They'll let you through the gate and put you into isolation." Kane saw the concern on Mo's face growing with each word spoken.

"Should we go into isolation now?"

Kane shook his head. "Not until we confirm things. Right now, it's just speculation. We need some proof and even then there should be no way they know of your involvement. This is all just a precaution in case something goes wrong. If I get any sense that there's a danger for you or your family, I'll let you know. If you get my coded call, then you grab those go bags and you leave right away."

"And the permits for my family and me to come to America?"

Kane sighed, his shoulders slumping. "I don't know, my friend. I'm trying my best, but ironically, this intel that has me so concerned if it proves true, might just be your ticket out of here."

Mo chuckled. "So, what you're saying is, what you think might get me killed just might save my life."

Kane flashed a smile. "That's about it."

"Shouldn't you be off saving the world somewhere, you lazy bum?"

Kane twisted to see Niner striding toward him, a broad smile on his face, flanked by five buddies from Bravo Team. He rose and handshakes with thumping hugs were exchanged. "I was expecting Charlie Team, what with it being Dax."

Dawson nodded. "It was decided they were too close to it, so they sent us instead."

"So, they sent the B team."

"Hey, that's Bravo Team," snapped Niner. His eyes narrowed. "Wait a minute. Do you think they were called the A-Team because they were actually Alpha Team?"

Kane shrugged. "I have no idea, but you're definitely Murdock."

Niner flipped him the bird.

"Hey, BD! Is that you?"

Everybody turned to see the Aussie pilot striding toward them. Dawson's head tilted to the side. "Ben?"

"In the flesh, my friend."

"I didn't recognize you with hair." Dawson greeted the man with a hearty handshake and a slap on the shoulder. "My God, you dropped off the face of the earth. I thought you were dead."

"I almost was, mate. Damn car accident."

Dawson chuckled. "With the crazy shit I've seen you pull, I figured you would have broken your neck skydiving naked out of an airplane."

"Second most fun you can have with your clothes off." Ledger jerked a thumb toward Kane. "So, you know this guy?"

"Unfortunately."

"Huh. I didn't realize you were in the insurance business."

Dawson laughed. "Yeah, I met him when I was having my yacht insured. Gave me a good deal."

"I figured he was Bragg or the Farm. Now I guess I have my answer."

"Or do you?"

Ledger's eyebrows shot up. "Oh, he was poached? Huh, I guess they've lowered the bar. I had to save your buddy's ass today."

"That's not how I remember it," protested Kane.

Ledger eyed him. "I had to leave the airstrip under fire, then land on a poor excuse for a road to rescue your ass."

Kane stared him straight in the eye. "This is Afghanistan. Those people could have just been celebrating you departing on schedule for a change with a friendly volley of gunfire into the air. And I think if you ask the locals, that road you landed on is simply the secondary runway. You picked me up because you realized you had forgotten to wait for two of your passengers."

Ledger turned to Dawson. "Is he always like this?"

Dawson rolled his eyes. "You can see why we were happy when he left."

Kane tapped his heart with a clenched fist twice. "That cut deep, BD. I'm feeling a little verklempt." He faked a stifled sob and bit a knuckle.

Niner rushed forward and leaped through the air, wrapping his arms and legs around Kane's torso. "Don't listen to him, Dylan. He doesn't speak for all of us." He threw in a few good hip thrusts.

Kane pulled Niner off him, holding him out like a slobbering puppy, Niner's feet dangling in the air. "You'd figure after all these years you guys would have housebroken him by now."

Atlas grunted. "I suggested neutering, but the Colonel shut me down."

Kane lowered Niner to the ground and held up a finger to him. "Behave."

Niner whimpered and Spock's eyebrow shot up. "I would have thought having a girlfriend would have tamed him a bit."

Niner gave him a look. "I'll have you know that Angela loves it when I do that to her."

Kane eyed Niner. "The girl must be a saint."

"That's the only conclusion we've been able to come up with," said Sergeant Gerry "Jimmy Olsen" Hudson. "I keep asking her to blink twice if she's being held against her will, but she never does."

A Humvee pulled up and a corporal stepped out, walking over to the group, uncertain who to address as no one had rank insignia. "Excuse me, gentlemen. I'm Corporal Fayette. I understand you have an Afghan national that requires an escort."

Kane acknowledged the young man then turned to Mo, already on his feet, bag in hand. "This is your passenger. Arrange a local ride for him, *trusted* local ride, inside the wire. I don't want anybody outside seeing him on base. Understood?"

"Yes, sir. I'll see to it personally."

"Good." Kane gave Mo a handshake. "Be careful, and remember everything I said. Be prepared to leave on a moment's notice."

"I understand. You be careful too."

Kane slapped the man on the shoulder and tilted his head toward the waiting vehicle. "Get your butt out of here and enjoy that birthday party."

Mo flashed a smile and climbed in the back of the Humvee, the corporal closing the door then settling in behind the driver's seat before pulling away. Mo waved, his fear evident.

"Do you think you're going to be able to get them out?" asked Dawson.

Kane shook his head. "No idea. Tens of thousands of applications have just been sitting there. We promised these people we'd take them out with us. If we never intended to do it, then we shouldn't have made the promise and led these people on. Everyone in Washington knows that as soon as we pull out, this country is going to shit and it's going to shit fast. And every single one of them that worked for us will be singled out and killed along with their families. It's going to be a blood bath."

"Well, if the Russians are involved in this, that might be his ticket out."

Kane agreed. "That's what I just told him a few minutes ago, but if the Russians are involved, we could be going to war, and none of what we did here will matter."

Operations Center 2, CIA Headquarters

Langley, Virginia

"We've got a hit!" announced Tong, who then held up a finger. "Correction. We've got multiple hits!" She pointed at the displays at the front of the room, three files showing with headshots, their records scrolling underneath.

"What am I looking at?" asked Leroux as he rose from his station and stepped closer to the screens.

"These are the three that were found in Akhtar's house when the authorities arrived. Two were shot dead, one killed in an explosion. Their bodies were stripped of any identification which suggests there were others involved in the execution of Akhtar and his family that survived the attack."

Child spun in his chair. "They sure don't look like the photos we were sent. Those bodies had full beards and long hair. They were full-on fundamentalist."

Tong tapped at her keyboard and a moment later the headshots were displayed alongside the crime scene photos. "Give them a haircut and a shave, and they're the same guys. Their fingerprints have been confirmed. Meet Khasi Varayev, Takhir Aslanbekov, and Alty Charyeva, all known mercenaries. Varayev and Aslanbekov are from Chechnya, loyal to the Russian-supported government. They served in their forces for five years in the same unit, then left and went private. Charyeva is from Turkmenistan. Private for as long as we've got files on him."

"Chechnya and Turkmenistan? Interesting. Both former Soviet territories, both with Russian-friendly governments."

"And with their ethnicity, they all look the part if they just skip the barber. Perfect candidates if you want to run an op in Afghanistan. They're not technically Russian, so if they're caught, Moscow can deny any involvement."

"Okay, let's see if we can trace their movements. Also, I want any known associates of theirs circulated. My guess is they're cleaning up before pulling out. Let's get photos out to all the airports in the area. And have the computer slap some beards on them as well."

"You got it," replied Tong, immediately going to work.

Child stared at the ceiling, slumped in his chair. "Is this the smoking gun we've been looking for?"

Leroux shook his head. "Not yet, but we're getting closer."

Child frowned. "What's going to satisfy Washington?"

"A signed confession," chirped Therrien from the back.

Leroux chuckled. "That would help, but I don't even know if that would be enough. We're talking Russia, not Syria. Even if we had irrefutable proof, Washington's likely to want to go to the UN about it rather than target Russian assets and risk escalating the situation."

Child grunted. "I say the hell with it. Escalate. These bastards killed our men and women. They don't deserve to escape just because they have nuclear weapons."

Leroux sat. "I agree with the sentiment, which is why I'm happy decisions like that are above my pay grade." He chewed his cheek for a moment. "The President's going to want to target something very specific that sends a message."

"Who? Like the guy behind it?"

Leroux shrugged. "The guy behind it could be the big man himself."

"Yeah, but he's not going to get his hands dirty. Take out the one who carried out the orders, and maybe the big guy gets the message not to do it again."

Leroux pursed his lips. "Have we got anything more from Echelon on that Moscow number that was dialed?"

Child checked the system and shook his head. "No, beyond that first brief call, everything else to that number has come in from local numbers, all encrypted."

"And our code breakers haven't been able to make out anything about the phrase that was said in that call?"

"No, the last report is that they couldn't find anything in their recent intercepts with that phrase, but they're looking deeper. 'Albatross is a go.' What the hell is an albatross anyway?"

"It's a type of bird."

"I think it's also a double eagle in golf," added Therrien.

Child scratched his armpit. "So, a bird around your neck is supposed to indicate what? Hardship?"

Leroux chewed his cheek at the colloquialism, an albatross around your neck. It was something that dragged you down, inhibited your progress, a burden. If Afghanistan were anything, it was definitely an albatross for America. Twenty years of constant fighting, of countless lives. The question had been posed earlier once the Russian connection had been suggested. What would they gain? The hostilities between the two countries were heating up, but in no way was it at the level where openly murdering each other's troops was on the agenda. Yet if they were employing mercenaries, it wasn't that overt, as they were making an effort to hide what they were doing.

But what was their motivation? What would killing American troops accomplish beyond simply killing American troops? Taking out several dozen of your old Cold War enemy accomplished nothing in a numbers game in the millions. If you removed Russia from the equation and looked at it purely as if it were the Taliban attacking, which was what everyone had been made to believe, then what did that accomplish?

Tong folded her arms and leaned back as Leroux continued to think. "All these attacks, especially where they're happening in peaceful areas, could they be wanting to destabilize these other regions?"

Leroux's head bobbed as he was pulled out of his internal debate. "That's what I was thinking as well. Keep killing our troops repeatedly, make it look like the Taliban are doing it in areas where they're not supposed to be that well organized, and it makes it look like they're operating with impunity throughout most of the country."

"But what does that gain the Russians?" asked Child.

Tong's eyes shot wide as her jaw dropped. "It's revenge!"

Everyone stopped what they were doing and Leroux turned his chair to face her. "Revenge for what?"

"For what we did in the eighties. We supplied the Mujahideen with weapons, including Stinger missiles. They were shooting helicopters and airplanes out of the sky, blowing up tanks. Thousands of Soviet soldiers died because we supplied the weapons."

"Yeah, but that was over thirty years ago," said Child. "And the Soviet Union doesn't exist anymore."

"Doesn't it?" Leroux rose and paced, his arms folded, a lone finger tapping on his chin. "The Russian president is former KGB. He thinks the greatest tragedy to have ever befallen the world is the collapse of the Soviet Union, and he's doing everything he can to restore it. The only real difference between the Soviet Union and today's Russia is that they have embraced capitalism. Anything America did to the Soviet Union in the past will be treated by him as if it were done to today's Russia. He doesn't make a distinction between the two. Russia is the Soviet Union just by a different name. He could be trying to inflict as much pain on us before we leave where his beloved Soviet Union was defeated."

"But why now, why wait so long?"

"Because we're leaving. This is their last chance to get revenge, but if they're truly successful, they might be thinking we'll delay our drawdown because the country isn't stable enough for us to leave."

Child grunted as he spun in his chair. "And if we don't leave, they keep killing us."

"Exactly. Either way, they win."

"So, what do we do about it?"

"We keep looking for that proof so Washington can decide how they want to respond. For now, let's keep tracking that phone in Moscow, start cross-referencing its locations against known members of the Kremlin inner circle. We might get lucky."

Therrien cleared his throat. "I might have something here."

"What's that?" asked Leroux.

"When we found out about the attack on Akhtar's house and the fact that three of the hostiles were killed, it got me thinking they might want to abort, especially if they aren't locals, and the quickest way out of Afghanistan is by air. I've got four last-minute tickets, all bought within fifteen minutes of each other, all under different names, different credit cards."

"Any IDs?"

"Just the names on the tickets. I'm running them now."

"If it is the Russians, even if they're fake, it's probably going to be hard to tell," said Tong.

Leroux agreed. "When does that flight leave?"

"Thirty minutes."

"Then we better act fast."

Hamid Karzai International Airport
Kabul, Afghanistan

Dawson, Atlas, Spock, and Jagger approached the rear of the Airbus A220 idling on the tarmac, the pilot ordered to wait for a VIP passenger. The stairs were still pushed up against the front door and were the single way inside. They had received the orders to hit the plane less than half an hour earlier, and a Black Hawk had dropped them off only minutes ago.

There had been no time to plan the op the way they usually would. Fortunately, they trained for these scenarios all the time on different types of airplanes, including this one. Everyone on his team knew the layout, knew the blind spots, knew exactly what arc they were covering, so they could all rush forward, shooting, without risking hitting each other or leaving any hostiles uncovered.

Fifty-four civilians were on board, four of whom were their targets, though there could be more, and there was still a chance these men they were after were innocent. Their aim wasn't to go in and shoot them all, their aim was to secure them for questioning. If, however, their targets attempted to engage, his team's ROEs allowed them to respond with lethal force.

They reached the rear of the fuselage, unseen by any passengers, though if anyone were observing the airport, they could phone in a warning, which was why cellphone jammers had been deployed the moment they arrived.

He activated his comms. "One-One, Zero-One. Any sign of activity, over?"

"Negative, Zero-One. All I'm seeing are pissed-off passengers, over," replied Niner from a sniper's nest atop the airport terminal with Jimmy. The likelihood of them being able to help was minimal if the battle remained on board, but if it took a turn for the worse and ended up outside the plane, they could prove invaluable.

"Copy that, One-One. Making entry now." Dawson surged toward the stairs, hugging the fuselage so anyone peering out a window wouldn't see him. He broke away, heading for the foot of the stairs then raced up them with the others on his heels, his Glock at the ready. The aircraft's layout was seared in his mind, the seat numbers assigned to their targets overlaid on the image of what he was about to face. Their targets were scattered about the cabin on both sides of the aisle, front to back. His job was to secure the one at the rear so those behind him wouldn't have to struggle past him to get to theirs.

He cleared the hatch and turned right, sprinting down the aisle shouting, "United States Military! Everybody stay put and raise your hands!"

Half those on board followed the orders, the other half either didn't, or didn't understand them. He reached his target and aimed his weapon squarely at the man's chest, recognizing him from the security footage taken when the man checked in. He ignored the shouts behind him as the others secured their targets.

"Allahu Akbar!" shouted someone behind him and Dawson cursed then flipped his weapon around, grabbing it by the muzzle and pistol-whipping his target. Gunshots rang out before he could turn. Spock stood, his Glock aimed at a seat. Dawson couldn't see the passenger, though there was little doubt Spock had shot him. Somebody leaped from across the aisle, grabbing for Spock's weapon, and Dawson fired two shots, both hitting the man squarely in the back, center mass. He dropped in a heap as Spock took two steps back. A man rose to Dawson's left and he coldcocked him, sending him back into his seat, blood trickling down his forehead.

And the passengers erupted in a mix of panic and rage.

Orders barked from the front of the plane, with a tone that had everyone, including him, turning toward the new masked arrival.

"Everybody calms down, now, or I'll give orders to shoot anyone who moves!"

Kane's order, delivered in Pashto, silenced most of those screaming and yelling at his former comrades. He adjusted the ski mask covering his face. "Good. Now we're going to be taking a few people from the plane for questioning, then you can continue on your way."

"Who do you think you are?" screamed a woman in English, seated near the front of the aircraft, dressed in Western attire.

Kane drew his weapon and aimed it at her. "I think I'm the man with the gun who has orders to kill anyone who interferes with the apprehension of potential terrorists." He tilted his head at Dawson's team. "Now these are American soldiers. They won't kill you. But my orders are different. I'm not an American soldier. Now I suggest you take your seat, shut your mouth, and let these men do their job trying to protect you. Otherwise, you'll get to see firsthand just how far my orders let me go."

The woman's face slackened as she dropped back into her seat defeated, called out on her arrogant presumption that because she was white she shouldn't be subjected to what was happening.

Kane turned to Dawson. "Well, that turned into a Charlie Foxtrot."

Dawson shrugged. "Shit happens. Two of our targets are still alive."

"Let's get our guys out of here. We need to contain this as quickly as we can before word gets out." Kane turned around and left the aircraft. Several dozen Afghan security personnel were waiting outside and he walked up to the colonel in charge. "Here's your story, Colonel. During an operation to arrest a known terrorist, he managed to open fire with a weapon smuggled on board. The terrorist was killed along with four men who attempted to intervene. Their names will be released once they've been identified and next of kin notified. The plane is grounded for the investigation, and the passengers will all be held for questioning for the next twenty-four hours to determine if they had any involvement. It's absolutely essential that nobody who witnessed that operation gets word out on what happened for one full day. Understood?"

"Yes, sir."

"Thank you, Colonel. Your allies appreciate your cooperation in this matter." Kane bowed his head slightly and spun on his heel, following Dawson and the others as they led the two surviving prisoners from the plane and toward a Black Hawk helicopter landing nearby. Kane climbed on board as hoods were fitted over the prisoners' heads. He extended a hand and hauled Niner into the back as Atlas did the same for Jimmy. The helicopter lifted off and banked away from the scene of the action as the Afghan security forces swarmed on board the now grounded aircraft.

"Well, that went about as expected," said Niner.

Dawson agreed. "Yeah, as soon as they figured out who we were after, I think they all decided they'd rather die than risk having Moscow think they were surrendering willingly."

Kane noticed one of the men tense at the mention of Moscow, and he played it up. "Well, the Kremlin's going to want to know why two of their guys are dead and why we have two in custody. I spoke to the local commander, and he's agreed to hold everybody for twenty-four hours, so by the time Moscow realizes these guys didn't arrive at their destination, they will have plenty of time to spill their secrets."

Dawson smiled slightly, picking up on what was going on. "And when you're done with them?"

"I haven't decided yet. It depends on how hard they make me work. Tell me what I want to know, and maybe I release them early so they can get a head start on their Kremlin buddies. Make me work for it, then the body count from what just happened might go up by two. It all depends. I think we've got two errand boys here. It's up to them whether they want to die for the people who revealed where we could find them."

One of the hoods spun toward him and Kane's smile spread. Not only did these men speak English like he suspected, but he could get a reaction out of them that quite often revealed more than words.

The next few hours could prove very interesting.

Briefing Room 3C, CIA Headquarters
Langley, Virginia

Leroux sat beside the Chief in a conference room filled with more CIA senior management than he had seen in a long time. At the front of the room, the displays showed a grid of DC and Pentagon senior officials, including the President.

Leroux was shaking, his nerves threatening to get the better of him. He had been in briefings like this before, usually a wallflower, though at times he had been required to speak. But this was different. The Chief had called this meeting, but there would be one person giving the briefing, one person answering the questions, including questions that might come from the President himself.

Him.

This was his briefing, and the decisions made here today could eventually lead to war.

Morrison was speaking now, saying something that was just a distant echo, and he felt overwhelmed, his chest tightening.

"Breathe," said Tong in his ear, her calming voice triggering him to inhale deeply, the action snapping him back to reality. He reached forward and grabbed his insulated mug, taking a drink of the ice-cold water it contained, thanking God Sherrie had cured him of his Red Bull habit, otherwise they would be prying him off the ceiling right now like a cartoon cat.

"So, I'll hand things over to one of my top analysts, Chris Leroux."

Morrison turned to Leroux and gave him a reassuring smile that didn't help one bit. Leroux took another drink of his water and inhaled again. "Thank you, Director Morrison. What follows is a summary of what my team and others, both at Langley and on the ground, have discovered during the course of our investigation. At this moment, what we are calling the Bounty Program, has been linked to seven separate ambushes on our people resulting in over thirty deaths, all while on missions in normally peaceful areas of Afghanistan.

"On two occasions, including the most recent attack, overhead drones caught footage of a man taking photos of the bodies of our soldiers. These were two different men. We've now been able to determine the purpose of the photos. This man on the screen"—an image of Akhtar appeared as Tong controlled the visual aspect of the presentation—"is Abu Mohammed Akhtar, a former Al-Qaeda lieutenant, once close to Bin Laden. Our intel tells us he was ejected from the organization shortly after nine-eleven. He apparently opposed the attacks, thinking our reprisals would be too great, and it would actually backfire on them. He's been out of their organization for almost twenty years, but we have photographic evidence, and eyewitness testimony, that he's one of the men behind the attacks on our troops.

"Ten thousand American dollars have been paid for each photograph of a dead American soldier. Akhtar would recruit locals, offer them the bounty, then if they expressed an interest, give them a phone. They would return to their village, recruit twelve people to participate, find out the time of the next scheduled American visit, then contact Akhtar with the details. Six men would show up the morning of the attack, arm then train the locals on how to use the weapons, then conduct the ambush.

"We now know that at least some of those men weren't Afghan. Once the attack was carried out, the local recruit would take his photos, then meet with Akhtar, who would then pay ten thousand per dead American soldier, plus a one-thousand dollar per head bonus to the recruit himself. Some of these bonuses were kept by the recruit, others were handed over to the village. Some even kept all the money for themselves. We have photographic evidence of large expenditures at the villages that cooperated in the attacks."

Tong cycled through photographs and drone footage, many in the room muttering curses at the obvious betrayal.

"After one of our operatives questioned one of the recruits, it was discovered that he had taken a photo of Akhtar for protection. After our operatives left, that recruit called Akhtar using a satellite phone that we've now been able to track using Echelon. In this conversation, the recruit indicated he had been visited by Americans and claimed it was our people who had his photo. Akhtar was quite agitated over this and over the phone call, no doubt because it could be traced.

"Yesterday, Akhtar and his family were found dead at his home in Kabul. Three other bodies were found at the scene that we assume were part of the team that carried out the attack. It's our belief that he informed his handlers of the security breach, and the attack on him was part of a clean-up operation.

"We were able to identify the three men. Two were Chechens, former members of the Russian Army. The other was from Turkmenistan. All are known mercenaries. With their identities, we were able to expand the search to known associates. One of my team discovered four last-minute tickets bought on a flight out of Kabul, all ordered separately, but within fifteen minutes of each other. It raised our suspicions, so we had a team on the ground board the plane. Two of the men were killed in the takedown, and the other two were taken into custody.

"Thanks to the cooperation of our Afghan allies, this news hasn't gotten out yet. Everyone on that plane is being held. All that those behind this will know is that their people didn't arrive at their destination. A story has been put out that during the arrest of a single terrorist on that plane, multiple people were killed, so for now, whoever is behind this won't know for sure what's happened. During interrogation, one of the men broke and confirmed the disturbing details I'm about to give you."

Leroux wiped the sweat off his forehead and took a swig of his water. This was the moment. It had been kept quiet until now. Other than his team, the Chief, Kane, and some of Bravo Team, no one else knew what he was about to say. "Once we had the phone number that Akhtar was using to coordinate the attacks, we were able to determine the phone number of his handler, and thanks to Echelon, we have transcripts of most of those calls, confirming which attacks he was involved in.

"Akhtar would provide his contacts with the locations and dates of the attacks, and then there'd be no further communication until the attack was complete and the number of photos was confirmed. That indicates that the handlers were the ones supplying the six men that would arrive before each attack, and supplying the bounty money to Akhtar when the job was completed. Also, note that Akhtar was receiving an equal amount, ten thousand a head.

"We then traced the handler's phone number. All calls were to or from Akhtar, except for the very first call made three months ago after it was activated. And that's where this gets very concerning."

Those in the room leaned forward and the faces in the cameras grew.

"That first number that was called was a cellphone located in Moscow."

Collective gasps erupted around him at the revelation.

"Are you telling me the Russians are behind this?" asked one of the faces on the display.

Morrison held up a finger. "Please hold your questions until the end of the briefing."

Leroux continued, his confidence growing as those around him hung on his every word. "Once we had that number, we began tracing it. We've been able to determine that it's a burner phone activated about four months ago. All calls to and from it, except for this one call, are encrypted. In that call, which lasted only six seconds, Echelon intercepted the conversation. In Russian, the person placing the phone call said, 'Albatross is a go,' and the person receiving the call, in Russian, replied, 'Good luck.' And then the call was terminated. We've been able to trace the location of this phone all over Moscow, including…" He paused as he gulped and reached for his water, then decided against it, instead delivering the bombshell that everyone was impatiently waiting to hear. "Including repeatedly on the Kremlin grounds, suggesting that this person either works there, or has near-daily contact with those who do."

The room erupted in shock and anger. Faces disappeared from the cameras and Leroux grabbed his water then leaned back as a map of Moscow was shown on the display. Various locations they had been able to trace the phone to were highlighted, and a large red arrow pointed to a swath of Russia's capital city with 'Kremlin' spelled out in bold letters, indicating a cluster of dozens of phone calls made or received on its grounds.

Morrison leaned closer to him. "You're doing a great job. Keep it up."

Air burst from Leroux's lips, causing them to vibrate. "I just want it over with."

Morrison chuckled. "Son, we haven't even gotten to the questions yet. And if they agree with you that it's the Russians, and they decide to go with the plan you and Kane cooked up, we could be here all day and night."

Leroux's shoulders slumped. "Well, I've got nothing but an empty home to go to, so I might as well stick around."

Sheremetyevo Alexander S. Pushkin International Airport
Moscow, Russia

Sherrie White stood outside the arrivals area, her cover that of an excited Canadian tourist waiting for her boyfriend to arrive. She was relatively new to the spy game, but because she spoke fluent Russian, Russia was one of her assigned zones. She wasn't exactly sure what the mission was, except that she was here to assist Kane. When the Chief had called her into headquarters, her boyfriend was there in Morrison's office, where she was told almost nothing. They were sending her to Moscow to rendezvous with Kane, though the operation hadn't yet been approved. The meeting to decide that was starting in half an hour. They wanted her in the air just in case it was approved so she'd be in position to assist.

She knew Leroux well enough to know he was nervous, that whatever this was, was serious, and Morrison was concerned too.

Normally meetings like that had him behind his desk, but instead, the three of them were in the seating area of his office where there were several chairs and a couch.

"This mission could be extremely dangerous. If it's approved, Dylan will fill you in on the details."

"So, you can't tell me anything?"

Morrison shook his head. "No. If the operation isn't approved, the fewer people that know we were even considering it, the better. There's only a handful of people who know what's being considered. Even in the meeting we're about to attend, once it's agreed that certain parties are involved, most will be excused from the meeting to discuss our response. Trust me when I say, if we don't go ahead with this, you don't want to know about it, because if it ever leaks, a clean-up might be conducted, and I wouldn't want your career impacted."

She glanced over at Leroux with concern. "What about Chris?"

Morrison chuckled. "He could be as screwed as I could be, but I'll try to protect him as much as I can. I'll insist that I had him and Dylan come up with the plan under my orders."

She wanted to know what the plan was, desperately wanted to know, but they had told her nothing. Even in her private goodbye with Leroux, he refused to reveal anything.

"When you find out what's going on, you'll understand."

"And if I don't find out?"

"Then be happy you didn't."

It had driven her crazy on the entire flight to Moscow, and the three-hour wait in one of Moscow's finest hotels. The first indication the operation was a go was the tap at her hotel room door 90 minutes ago. It was a coded knock that had her both tense and at ease. Adrenaline momentarily fueled her, but she quickly got it under control and opened the door. A blond woman with model good looks pleasantly smiled at her.

"We found your missing luggage." The woman pushed a large suitcase into the room. "We regret the inconvenience."

Sherrie returned the smile, pulling the suitcase deeper inside. "Not a problem. These things happen. At least I got it before my plans for this evening."

"Enjoy your stay in Moscow." The woman smiled then walked away, nothing else said. Sherrie closed the door then heaved the heavy suitcase onto her bed. It was obviously a delivery from Langley, as she wasn't missing any luggage. She dialed in her personal three-digit code on the tiny lock holding the zippers together, then yanked at it. It opened and she tossed it on the bed, then unzipped the suitcase, flipping the lid open.

And gasped at what was inside.

An M24 Sniper Weapon System.

It could mean only one thing. They were here to assassinate someone. But what didn't make sense was why this particular weapon? It was American. Any forensic analysis after the fact would determine the type of weapon used. Why wouldn't they use something Russian, something Chinese, something that at least had some chance of deflecting suspicion away from America?

She growled. She had no idea what was going on. With so little information, all she could do was guess, and that wouldn't help anyone. She had searched the rest of the suitcase, finding it packed with the tools of the trade including fake IDs, passports, and a travel itinerary for a flight leaving in six hours. Whatever was going to happen was going to happen soon. She took a little comfort in the knowledge that she might be safely out of the country before the day was over, or dead, and her worries would be over.

A small comfort.

This was the job. She could get killed on any mission. She had accepted that life, but she had accepted it before she met Leroux. Now she had someone she cared about, someone she loved, someone she wanted to have a family with, grow old with. But she also didn't want to give up her job. She was too young. Barring injury, she had a minimum of 15 good years left in her, though it would be pushing the upper limits of an active agent. Forty-year-old legs simply couldn't outrun a 25-year-old opponent. But lots of agents switched their roles as they got older to less active missions, to things more covert rather than overt. Perhaps when she made that switch, then they could have a family.

Kane stepped through the arrival area doors and beamed a smile at her, which she returned, in character. This wasn't the first time they had played boyfriend and girlfriend, and because they were good friends in real life, not to mention the fact he was gorgeous, it made their bit of play-acting that much easier. She just hoped Leroux wasn't watching on a hacked camera, because she knew how she'd feel if the roles were reversed—insanely jealous. But if this operation were as covert as she had been led to believe, there was no way Langley would risk hacking anything they didn't absolutely need to. Kane's safe arrival could be easily confirmed with a lookout.

Kane let go of his luggage cart and grabbed her in a bear hug, lifting her off the floor before planting a kiss on her that had her weak in the knees. "I missed you."

"I missed you more. Did you get all your luggage?"

He patted the cart. "Yeah."

"They lost one of mine," she said as they headed toward the doors. "But they found it. It arrived a little over an hour ago."

"Well, that's good. We can't exactly see the sights if you've got nothing to wear."

No looks were exchanged, no winks, no secret handshakes. There was no doubt there were cameras on them. The question was, were the cameras on everyone, and the footage of them would be looked at after the fact, or were the cameras already on them specifically, because the Russians knew what was coming?

They walked over to the taxi stand and the cabby loaded Kane's bags in the trunk. They climbed in and were soon underway. The fact they had made it this far meant nothing. If they were under surveillance, the Russians would want to catch them in the act, catch them somewhere with their target in their sights, their American weapons in hand.

And the propaganda coup would be massive.

In fact, it might just save their lives.

Kane took her hand and squeezed it, still in character. "I love this city. There's just something about it that we don't have back home in Canada. There's so much history here."

The cabby glanced in the mirror. "You're from Canada?"

Kane nodded. "We both are. Ottawa."

"I would love to visit Canada someday. I have relatives there in a place called Winnipeg. Have you heard of it?"

Kane smiled. "Of course. Capital of Manitoba. Flattest city you'll ever find, and winters that'll make you miss Siberia."

The cabby roared with laughter. "So, are you two here for the parade?"

Kane's grip tightened slightly, indicating she should remain quiet. "Not specifically, but we'll probably check it out. Nobody puts on a parade like the Russians."

The cabby agreed emphatically. "As soon as I drop you off at your hotel, I'm done for the day. I'm going to pick up my wife and children, and make sure we get a good spot along the route."

"I'd like to get close to the grandstand if I can. See the president and all those generals with their ribbons. It's impressive."

The cabby chuckled. "It's very hard to get anywhere close to that. You usually have to be connected. And don't be too impressed by the ribbons. The Russian Army loves to give them out. My father says some of those generals got a ribbon for being able to shit in a hole, and a second one for remembering to wipe." The man roared in laughter at his own joke.

Kane and Sherrie joined in as they pulled up to the hotel, leaving her wondering if Kane's mentioning of the grandstand was significant. Could their mission be to assassinate someone who would be standing there today? She suppressed the urge to gulp. Could their target be the Russian president himself? Her heart raced into overdrive at the implications.

If that were the case, there was no way they were getting out of here alive.

Magdanly, Turkmenistan

Dawson had interrogated prisoners before but was always bound by strict rules that prevented him from beating the living shit out of someone to get the information he needed. He usually had to rely on intimidation and pretend that he'd unleash Atlas on them if the prisoner didn't cooperate. Atlas would then growl, flex his upper-body muscles, and most would spill if they weren't highly trained. If they were, more often than not, he would hand them over for further interrogation, where if it were outside of Gitmo, they would break them through standard techniques that were still permitted. Some would never break, and too often, those who did were simply spouting whatever the interrogator wanted to hear.

In this case, he and Atlas had stood behind Kane, still masked up, Atlas' arms, chest, and shoulders bulging as he glared at the one who had reacted in the chopper. Dawson merely delivered his thousand-yard stare, boring into the man's soul, while Kane sat across from the man with a tablet computer in his hand.

"Your name is Zura Shishani. You were born in Grozny, Chechnya on September 23rd, 1985. You joined the Russian Army in 2004, served for eight years, seeing a lot of action in Chechnya, then was honorably discharged, and within a year was a gun for hire." Kane wagged the tablet. "I know everything about you. I know you've got family, and I know you do the Russian government's dirty work. And I also know you're just a foot soldier. Bounty programs that pay ten thousand a head for each dead American soldier aren't set up or even run by people like you. So, here's what's going to happen. In less than twenty-three hours, everyone on that airplane will be released, including you and your friend. There's going to be footage released to the media showing me shaking your hand, thanking you for your cooperation, and you'll be walking out of here without a mark on your face. That footage is going to get back to Moscow within minutes.

"Within two hours of that, they'll have picked up your family, your friends, everybody that's important to you, because they can't risk this operation being traced back to them. You know the implications. If it became officially known what was happening, it could lead to war, and your taskmasters can't risk that. That's why they hired people like you to do their dirty work, and you hired locals. So, you're going to tell me everything you know. I want names, places, dates, phone numbers, how you were recruited, how you were paid, where was your first point of contact, where did you get resupplied, how did you get your money to pay off the bounties. I want to know everything, and if I feel you've told me all you know, then your name will be added to the list of the dead from that attack. We'll get you out of the country, and you'll at least have a fighting chance, and your family and friends may just go untouched. Don't cooperate"—Kane leaned forward with a smirk— "and I'll let you live."

The man had spilled for the better part of an hour. He had been recruited through a former Army buddy, the deposit sent to a Swiss bank account he already had set up for previous mercenary work, instructions dropped off that led him to a rally point in Syria where he met the rest of the team. They were given the mission details by men in plain clothes, all Russian. No names had been used, but his old buddy recognized one of the men, an officer he had once served under, Lieutenant Colonel Leonid Talanov.

Langley, who had been monitoring the interrogation, had sent a photo of Talanov to Kane's tablet and their prisoner had confirmed it was the same man, the leader of a brutal Spetsnaz unit known as Ghost Watch. He was active Russian Special Forces, and it had confirmed their worst fears.

This was indeed a Russian operation.

It might still be rogue, but Russians were actively involved that had the power to not only fund and supply the mission, but to provide an actual Spetsnaz unit. It meant someone on the inside. The question was who was that person, and was the Russian president aware of what was going on?

Hopefully, they were about to find out.

If all went according to plan.

Unfortunately, this mission was more likely to go according to expectations. These were highly-trained special forces they were going up against, some of the best in the world who were fully aware of the implications should their secrets be revealed. They wouldn't be going down without a fight, and Colonel Clancy had already told him that if the choice were between capturing one of the Russians and risking the life of one of his men, there was no choice.

The Russian died.

Right now, a coordinated effort was underway. They had the names of all the local recruits. Two were already dead, one by Kane's hand, the other in Kane's presence. The rest would be dead before the day was out, teams deployed across Afghanistan to carry out the President's orders. The locals the recruits had used to help them couldn't be identified for certain, so they would be left alone. However, anything that appeared to be new purchases from the time between the ambush and today would be confiscated or destroyed.

No one would profit from the death of an American soldier.

Their prisoner had confirmed that Akhtar was the only local they had involved directly, and the entire ground team of seven were now either dead or captured. All that remained were the Spetsnaz unit, and whoever was coordinating this from Moscow.

And Kane had a plan for identifying who that was.

Bravo Team's mission was to capture the Spetsnaz team if possible, eliminate them if necessary. Washington ideally wanted confessions on video in case the Russians decided they didn't want to cooperate with Kane's plan.

Dawson stared at his tablet, displaying footage from a camera set up by Niner and Jimmy, who had an elevated sniper position with a clear view of the walled-in backyard of the house the Russians were using to run their mission from. He activated his comms. "One-One, Zero-One. I'm seeing six subjects. Confirm?"

"Confirmed, Zero-One," replied Niner. "I count six targets."

"Is Colonel Talanov one of the six?"

"Affirmative, Zero-One. He's the one on the right of your image with his back to you. He turned around a moment ago and I got a good look at his face."

"Good. He's the one we want. If anyone knows who the Moscow contact is, it'll be him." Dawson slipped the tablet into an inner pocket. "Control, Zero-One. Are we a go?"

"Stand by, Zero-One. Still awaiting confirmation from Diggler, over," replied Leroux in his ear.

Dawson gripped his M4, drawing in several deep, controlled breaths, settling down the adrenaline desperate to unleash itself on his system. His inclination was to simply blow up the entire compound then make certain everyone was dead. But those weren't his orders.

Yet.

The Ritz-Carlton
Moscow, Russia

Russians loved their parades. It was a holdover from their Soviet Union past that their current elected dictator loved. The former KGB strongman was the laughingstock of the West, the propaganda his people pumped out about him sometimes outright insane. Did anyone seriously believe that a 68-year-old man could score nine goals against former NHL players? His moments were so obviously staged, it was amazing how many of the population bought it.

But these people were now conditioned to distrust the West. The press was controlled, any opposition quelled. He won their elections in landslides, yet the rules were such that it was almost impossible for an opposition party to register. Ballot boxes were stuffed, votes were changed, and if anyone accused his party of committing voter fraud, they were dismissed as puppets of the West merely attempting to discredit a legitimate election because they were afraid of a strong Russia.

And the West *was* afraid of a strong Russia, but there was no longer any will to counter them. Over 30 years had gone by since the collapse of the Soviet Union, an entire generation having no concept of the danger the world faced during the Cold War, an entire generation that embraced socialism with no understanding of what communism was. Russia with its oil money was too powerful, and countries like Germany were willing to ignore history, including recent history, embracing a natural gas pipeline fed by Russia that would heat the homes of Europeans, a pipeline that could be shut down at any moment should the Russians take offense to something Europe said or did.

Russia could take over disputed territories around the world and nothing would be done about it. There would be protests by the politicians, America might send more troops into the area, the Europeans would threaten sanctions, and Russia would just turn the taps off. No one was going to war. No one could win, not without horrendous consequences. Wars today involving the major powers like the United States, Russia, and China, would be wars fought through political brinkmanship, cyber warfare, and economic warfare.

Yet there would be tit-for-tat exchanges like what was happening right now. Russia had crossed a line, a line it mustn't be allowed to cross again, and everything was waiting in Afghanistan and Moscow on Kane, right now lying prone on a table pushed in front of the window of a hotel room rented in the names of two Canadian tourists, chosen specifically for its view, a room suddenly opening up when the guests who had booked it somehow missed their flight. The few dozen people in the world who were aware of what was about to happen were waiting for him to trigger the next stage of his plan.

They were outside the security perimeter set up for the parade, and unbeknownst to Sherrie until a few minutes ago, her room had been chosen specifically so he had a line of sight with the grandstand. It was a difficult shot, though he'd done it before at this distance, and God was on their side today, the winds almost non-existent.

He peered through his scope and smiled. "Here we go," he said, his voice calm, his heart steady. The events he was about to initiate could start a war, though he was convinced it was the only way to avoid one. A response had to be sent, but today he was a scalpel, not a sledgehammer, though the repercussions would be felt for years to come.

The grandstand quickly filled with the who's who of the Russian president's inner circle, lining up behind where the despot would stand. Where they were positioned, where the cameras would catch them, indicated their standing in the eyes of their dear leader. Those at the fringes were of little importance, but those directly behind the man, especially the few who would stand up with him as the parade marched past, displaying the might of the Russian military, were either the most loyal and trusted, or those owed the most for actions taken that required favors.

The audience roared as the man himself appeared.

"Control, Diggler. Ready on this end, over."

"Copy that, Diggler. We're ready on this end. All cameras are being monitored, over."

Kane's heart rate couldn't help but pick up a few beats, and he inhaled deeply, shutting down the adrenaline that could affect his shot. "Send the signal."

Magdanly, Turkmenistan

Dawson's chestnuts were roasting over the open fire between his legs. They had been waiting for fifteen minutes at this point with the vehicle turned off, no air conditioning running.

"Zero-One, Control. You're a go. I repeat, you're a go, over."

"Copy that, Control. Commencing operation now," replied Dawson. "One-One, Zero-One. We're a go. Stand by for my signal, over."

Niner confirmed immediately. "Copy that, Zero-One."

Dawson checked the mirrors. There were a few locals nearby, but the moment they spotted him and the others, they would vacate the area quickly. "Let's go." He stepped out of the vehicle and strode with purpose across the street and down the road toward their target building, Atlas beside him. Spock and Jagger broke off at the 1-2 corner of the building where they already knew there was a side door.

Dawson and Atlas took up position on either side of the front gate to the small courtyard. He pressed the panic button on the key fob and a moment later the alarm blared on their SUV.

"Zero-One, One-One. You've got their attention," said Niner. "The colonel just sent two of the guys to check it out. They've entered the house and they're armed, over."

"Copy that, One-One." Dawson pocketed the fob, retightening the suppressor on his Glock. This was the thinning-out phase of the operation. If they could take out these two men without the other four knowing, their job might just get a little easier.

Footfalls echoed across the courtyard. He stepped back, aiming his weapon toward the gate, Atlas doing the same on the other side. A hand gripped one of the wrought iron bars then a head poked through, searching for the source of the alarm, instead finding the barrel of Dawson's weapon pointed directly at him. The man's eyes bulged and Dawson squeezed the trigger as Atlas swung out from the wall, stepping in front of the gate, firing off two rounds.

"Clear," he whispered, Dawson saying the same.

"Bravo Team, Zero-One. Two targets down in the courtyard. One-One, report, over."

There was a pause then Niner said, "Stand by."

Dawson reached through the gate and swung aside the latch that held it closed at the center. He pushed it open slightly, ready for what would hopefully be a silent breach.

Instead, Niner cursed in his ear.

Niner focused in on a tablet computer that one of the Spetsnaz team had picked up off a table. The man peered at it for a moment then shouts erupted as he swung the tablet around so Colonel Talanov could see. Talanov leaped from his chair as Niner caught a glimpse of what appeared to be an overhead shot of the house.

"We've been made, Zero-One. I repeat, we've been made. I think they've got a drone overhead."

Jimmy rolled onto his back, aiming his Glock at the sky, searching for a target.

"Copy that, One-One. Engage, I repeat, engage, over."

"Engaging." But it was already too late. Two of the men were rushing inside the household, shouting in Russian.

"What the hell did he just say?" asked Jimmy as he continued to scan the sky.

Niner squeezed the trigger of his sniper rifle, red mist spraying on the wall as the lone available target was taken out. Talanov spun, staring in his general direction before sprinting for cover. The colonel wasn't on the immediate target list, but they had a bigger problem than a lack of targets in the backyard. He redirected his weapon toward the windows.

"Zero-One, One-One. We've got a problem. After the targets went ape-shit, they ran into the house yelling, 'Everybody wake up!'"

Dawson cursed at Niner's report. There had only been time for one satellite flyby, and Washington didn't want a drone over the area in case it tipped off the Russians. It meant they had gone in almost blind. The question now was, were they facing another two or twenty-two? He was guessing another half-dozen tops. The house wasn't big enough for much more, but more importantly, the Russians would want to keep this compartmentalized as much as possible, so they would have the minimum involved to carry out the mission. The question now was what to do? They had the element of surprise, but only for the next 30, perhaps 60 seconds.

He headed for the front door, still making his decision. Shouts from inside, all in Russian, a language he understood well, were urgent but not panicked. After all, this was a Spetsnaz team, and just like his team, he wouldn't expect anyone to panic in a situation like this. Shock and surprise would be expressed, absolutely, but not at the expense of getting ready to repel an attack.

And it changed the equation.

"Control, Zero-One. We're changing the mission unless countermanded. This is now a shoot-to-kill operation, otherwise we abort."

"Stand by, Zero-One," replied Leroux.

Dawson cursed.

We don't have time to stand by.

Operations Center 2, CIA Headquarters

Langley, Virginia

Leroux already knew what the answer should be, and he would have given it already if the Chief weren't standing next to him monitoring the situation. He turned to the man, who dismissed the question before it could be asked.

"This is your mission."

Leroux nodded and opened the channel. "Zero-One, Control. You're a go for change in mission priority. I repeat, you're a go. Over."

"Copy that, Control. Better send in the package, just in case."

"Roger that, Zero-One." He snapped his fingers at Tong who spoke quietly into her own mic, then gave a thumbs-up.

"ETA to package arrival, eight minutes," she said.

He adjusted his headset. "Zero-One, Control. You've got eight minutes to abort the package or exit, over."

"Copy that, Control," came Dawson's reply, an explosion and gunfire almost drowning out the Delta operator.

Leroux said a silent prayer then turned his attention to the display that showed an image taken earlier of the target site, and six red dots, each tracking one of the Delta team members, their life sign indicators stacked on the left of the display, all showing heart rates elevated, though probably 10 to 20 beats per minute less than his own. These were the best of the best, but they were going up against Russia's best, outnumbered. He just prayed this wouldn't be one of the missions where he lost somebody because of his intel.

Child interrupted his train of thought. "Moscow Station is reporting. They've successfully pinged the phone, and they've confirmed the location."

Everyone in the room forgot for a moment what was happening on the other side of the planet with men they had worked with for years. This was the moment of truth.

"And?" asked Leroux.

"They're indicating they believe the phone is in the parade square."

Kane switched channels on his comms. "Diggler, this is Control. Moscow Station has confirmed they believe the phone is in the parade square, over."

"Copy that, Control. Stand by to make the phone call, and let me know the moment Bravo Team is clear. We want our message to be accurate."

Magdanly, Turkmenistan

Niner peered through his scope at Talanov, still in the backyard, as the man pulled out a phone. With the change in mission priority, the colonel was now a target. Niner could put a round through the man's chest, yet there was still an opportunity to take him as a prisoner. Unfortunately, that phone sealed the man's fate.

"Taking the shot."

He squeezed the trigger, relegating Talanov to the history books, then switched his focus to the windows as did Jimmy, his spotter, lying beside him, his M4 at the ready, having given up trying to find the drone overhead.

"Don't shoot with that thing unless it's necessary," said Niner. "Just tell me the shots."

"Second floor, far-right window."

Niner adjusted, spotting someone peering out the window. Niner fired, not bothering with the usual reporting. This was no longer a sniper mission, this was active engagement.

"Rear door, backyard."

Niner adjusted again as the door was thrown open, two men emerging with submachine guns gripped in their hands. "A little help." He took out the one on the left as Jimmy fired several shots with his M4, two rounds finding their target as Niner put a third into the man for good measure. Gunfire sprayed their position and they both dropped behind the foot-high wall that surrounded the edge of the rooftop they were on. He activated his comms. "Zero-One, One-One. Our position's been made, over."

"Then get your asses out of there and into the fight. You two have been lying down on the job too long. Zero-One, out."

Niner rolled his eyes at Jimmy then they both shuffled back as the gunfire continued on their position. It was from the second floor of their target building, and below their vantage point, limiting the shooter's angle. Within moments, any threat to them was eliminated. Niner rose to a knee and gave Jimmy a look. "He does know we actually greased four guys from here, doesn't he?"

"Well, no, he doesn't, because you stopped reporting your kills."

Niner rose to his feet. "Huh, I guess there is a reason for all that nonsense."

Automatic weapons fire erupted from the back of the residence, silencing Niner's sniper rifle. If the man was as accurate as he normally was, it suggested four targets had been taken out, and Dawson assumed the colonel was in the mix. There would be no interrogations today, no prisoners, no witnesses to the atrocities committed in Afghanistan. And he was fine with that. As far as he was concerned, every single person involved should be eliminated.

To his left, through several walls, the reports of Glocks firing as well as Makarovs indicated a gun battle from Spock and Jagger's position. As long as he continued to hear their weapons, he wouldn't worry about them. If they needed help, they would radio it in. But he did need to know how many were down. As if reading his mind, Niner's voice came in over the comms.

"Zero-One, One-One. Secure from Overseer position. Heading to rear of target building. Confirming four targets down including the primary, over."

"Thanks for the late report, One-One. I'm having your pay docked."

Footfalls hammered down steps on the opposite side of the wall in front of them. He exchanged a look with Atlas, who readied his M4 carbine. Dawson stepped back from the wall to get a better angle on the door, his Glock aimed at the opening. The footfalls fell silent and Dawson cursed at the distinctive sound of the pin being pulled from a grenade. A hand appeared for a moment through the door frame and the RGD-5 grenade was tossed inside, the metal ball of death bouncing on the floor.

Dawson rushed toward it and the table that stood between them. He grabbed the heavy piece of furniture and tipped it over on its side, hitting the ground behind it as Atlas dove from his position, sliding backward, his M4 belching lead at the wall that at least one Russian was using as cover. Dawson reached out and grabbed Atlas, hauling him the rest of the way. The grenade detonated, the concussive force enormous in the confined space, and Dawson thanked God for the ear protection he wore. The table shoved against them as a ball of flame whipped around its edges and Atlas cried out.

Dawson was immediately concerned for his friend, the toughest man he knew, but for the moment, he couldn't tend to him. A hostile emerged in the door frame, his AK-74 swinging in ahead of him, the muzzle flashing with each round erupting from its barrel. Dawson calmly placed two rounds in the man's chest, readying for the next attack, but none came. He pushed to his feet, glancing to see Atlas still breathing and grasping his calf, a large shard of wood from the table embedded in it.

"You okay?"

Atlas gave him the stink-eye. "What do you think? My leg looks like it should make the Property Brothers demo day blooper reel."

Footfalls overhead indicated they still had more in the house to deal with. Gunfire rang down the stairwell and Dawson jerked back. It appeared their enemy was making a stand on the second floor, which suited him just fine.

"Control, Zero-One. ETA on that package?"

"Two minutes, Zero-One. Suggest you evac now."

"Roger that." Dawson eyed the big man on the floor as he examined his leg. "Bravo Team, Zero-One. Evac to containment positions, over."

A string of acknowledgments were quickly received as he fired several rounds blindly up the stairwell to make anyone upstairs think twice about coming down the steps. He extended a hand and Atlas grabbed it. Dawson hauled the big man to his feet and slung a muscled arm over his shoulders. They left through the door they came in, but the moment they reached the courtyard, gunfire from the second floor tore up the cobblestone in front of them.

Dawson pressed against the chipped and cracked stucco wall. "This is Zero-One. We're pinned down in the courtyard and Zero-Seven has a leg wound. We need some suppression fire on the second floor, front windows, over."

Spock immediately replied. "Zero-One, Zero-Five. I'm on my way. Stand by."

Dawson glanced at Atlas. "You ready for this?"

"No, carry me."

Dawson chuckled as he adjusted Atlas' arm, prepping for the race across the courtyard. "Control, Zero-One. ETA?"

"Sixty seconds, Zero-One."

"Bravo Team, Zero-One. Fall back to safety positions immediately, over."

Confirmations came through then gunfire from an M4 chirped to their right, bullets spraying against the walls and through the windows overhead as Spock provided the cover they needed.

"Let's go, big guy." Dawson pushed away from the wall and Atlas hopped one-legged beside him as they covered the short distance across the courtyard toward the closed front gate. A second M4 opened up, and the Russian positions' sporadic gunfire fell silent with the addition of Jagger's weapon. They were soon at the gate and Dawson reached forward and flipped the latch aside, yanking the wrought iron out of the way. As they stepped through and onto the street, they cleared the gate and reached the cover of the wall.

"This is Zero-One. We're clear. Everybody break away immediately."

"Zero-One, this is Control. You've got ten seconds."

"Copy that, Control." Dawson hauled his impossibly heavy friend toward their SUV farther down the street, but there was no way in hell they were making it. Not in ten seconds. Spock and Jagger burst from the alleyway just ahead and sprinted toward them. Spock took Atlas' other arm and Jagger grabbed Atlas by the legs, and together the three of them carried the wounded warrior as Leroux's voice echoed in Dawson's ear.

"Three, two, one…"

"Everybody down!" shouted Dawson, and they hit the deck hard as the AGM-84K SLAM-ER cruise missile slammed into the compound behind them. The eruption was enormous, the shock wave sending debris in all directions, the heat from the blast engulfing them as he held his breath to prevent searing his lungs should the momentary flash prove too hot.

And as quickly as it had begun, it was over. Though it wasn't. Car alarms, screams, the cries of terrified children, the continued sounds of the building behind them collapsing, along with secondary explosions from stored ordnance, wouldn't let anyone witness to this day forget the destructive power America could unleash on its enemies.

Dawson quickly assessed the situation around them as he took a knee. "Everybody good?"

"I'm good," replied Spock.

Jagger patted himself down and confirmed the boys were intact, giving a thumbs-up.

Atlas stared up at them from the ground. "I'm glad you guys are, but what about me?"

Spock cocked an eyebrow. "You do know that if you're injured twice on the same mission, you still only get one purple heart?"

Atlas flipped him the bird. "If I knew it was safe to do so, I'd yank this thing out of my damn leg and plunge it into your heart, though I don't think it would have any effect because you clearly don't have one."

Niner and Jimmy appeared, having to take a longer route from the rear of the now-destroyed building. "What the hell's going on here?" asked Niner, the concern for his best friend evident in his voice.

Atlas glanced over at Niner. "Spock's being mean to me."

Spock held up both hands. "Not true. I was just reminding him of the regs." He jutted his chin toward Atlas. "Why don't you go sport hump your buddy? That always seems to cheer him up."

Atlas shoved both hands in the air. "Get me up!"

Dawson laughed then helped Spock haul the big man to his feet as Jagger retrieved the SUV. Moments later, Atlas was loaded in the back and they were underway, driving past the scene of devastation. The compound where the Russian Spetsnaz unit had been holed up directing an operation that had led to the murder of dozens of American soldiers was flattened, a rubble-strewn crater where the home had once stood, several mangled bodies evident.

Justice.

Dawson activated his comms. "Control, Zero-One. Inform Diggler he can deliver his message."

Operations Center 2, CIA Headquarters
Langley, Virginia

"Copy that, Zero-One. Proceed to exfil point Alpha. Extraction team is en route. Control, out." Leroux switched frequencies as Morrison entered the room, waving off any acknowledgment. "Diggler, Control. Secondary operation a success. Ready to proceed with primary upon your signal, over."

Kane's reply was immediate. "Control, Diggler. Ready to proceed, over."

Leroux glanced at Tong. "Ping it again. Make sure it's still where we think it is."

Tong relayed the instructions to Moscow Station then moments later gave a thumbs-up. "Confirmed, the phone is still in the same area. It's impossible to pinpoint, but it's still pinging off the same towers."

The display curving across the front of the operations center held half a dozen images of the parade grandstand. Everyone in the room had their assigned angle to examine, the operations center now packed with every analyst that had been working the various shifts, everyone privy to what had been going on now observing.

"This is it, people." He snapped his fingers at Tong. "Make the call."

She tapped a key as Leroux adjusted his headset, his heart hammering harder than it ever had. He could be about to start a war, one that could go nuclear if it got out of hand. The call was played on the speakers overhead and rang three times as Leroux stared at the gathered privileged few, searching for any indication that someone was about to answer a phone.

"Camera three!" shouted Therrien, and Leroux adjusted his gaze to see someone reach in their pocket and pull out a phone.

"Control, Diggler. I've got him. Taking the shot."

Leroux stared at the image as Tong zoomed in on it, and as the pixelated face resolved into a crystal-clear image, his heart nearly stopped. "Diggler, Control. Abort! I say again, abort!"

The Ritz-Carlton

Moscow, Russia

Kane removed his finger from the trigger as he cursed. "Control, Diggler. Why are we aborting?"

"The person who answered the phone can't be our target," replied Leroux in his ear. "He's too young. We're running the ID now. Stand by."

"Too young?" asked Sherrie.

Kane peered through his scope again. From this distance, he couldn't make out the man's face well enough to say one way or the other. All he could confirm was the man's hair wasn't gray. But for all he knew, the man could be using the Russian equivalent to the Grecian Formula for Men. But Langley had better images and wouldn't abort without cause. If this were a young man, he could be the aide to the person actually behind this. Taking him out would send their target into hiding, perhaps never to be found. Justice had to be delivered, a message had to be sent, and that meant the proper target had to be eliminated.

"Diggler, Control. We've identified the man as Dmitri Sokov. He's the adjutant to General Utkin."

Kane knew the name, and it was who he suspected was behind this as soon as he found out Spetsnaz was involved, as the Russian Special Forces ultimately came under his command. He was a hardliner, fiercely loyal to the Russian president, and known for his brutality.

"Is he on that stage?"

"Stand by, Diggler, we're checking."

Kane readied himself again.

"Diggler, Control. He's behind the president, over his left shoulder, flanked by two civilian males, black suit, blue tie on the left, dark gray suit, red tie on the right."

Kane aimed directly at the Russian president, the temptation to shoot the man almost irresistible. But that would mean war. He adjusted slightly and spotted the two civilians flanking General Utkin.

"Copy that, Control. Behind the Russian president, military uniform, flanked by two men in suits, one black with blue tie, one dark gray with red tie. Am I cleared to take the shot?"

"Affirmative, Diggler, you're a go for the shot."

Kane checked his settings one final time, something he normally wouldn't do. They were correct, but this was the most important shot he had ever taken. "Now."

Sherrie leaned forward and yanked on a suction cup placed on the window earlier, pulling away a neatly cut circle of glass, giving him an unobstructed shot. He drew a deep breath and slowly exhaled as he squeezed the trigger, the rifle butt slamming into his shoulder. He readied for a second shot, but as he peered through his scope, it was clear it wasn't needed. Utkin had collapsed to his knees, a hole in his chest, blood rapidly staining his uniform. He was dead, though his brain might not know it yet.

Chaos erupted on the grandstand.

Kane rose and placed a fresh bullet atop a note he had written earlier on stationery from the hotel, the final part of their message delivered.

Operations Center 2, CIA Headquarters

Langley, Virginia

Cheers erupted as one of the cameras zoomed in on the corpse of General Utkin. Others showed security forces rushing the grandstand, the Russian president grabbed and taken to safety as others scrambled to get off the platform. It was pandemonium, signaling that part of the mission was complete. But now, as far as Leroux was concerned, the most crucial part began.

Coordinating the safe escape of his best friend and his girlfriend.

The question was, what would the Russian reaction be? At the moment, they wouldn't know who was responsible, though they would certainly lock down the city. He had wanted to arrange a foolproof means of escape. They could do it. They had done it before. But Kane had refused. He had his own plans, and they were plans that Leroux disagreed with, especially with Sherrie involved. Unfortunately, Morrison had okayed them.

"If it works, then we know it's over," he had said.

He turned to Tong. "Monitor their locations. I want a fix on them at all times. The moment we have any indication something's going wrong, I want every camera in Moscow hacked so we can see where they take them."

"You got it."

Morrison turned to him. "I'm going to go brief the President."

"Bravo Team is in friendly airspace," reported Therrien in the back. "The medic says their injured man will be fine."

Leroux gave a thumbs-up over his shoulder without turning, his eyes glued to a map of Moscow, two red dots showing the most important people in his life leaving the hotel. And he said a silent prayer that Kane's foolhardy plan didn't mean the death of both of them.

The Ritz-Carlton
Moscow, Russia

Agent Oleg Gridnev of the Russian FSB stepped into the hotel room and assessed the crime scene, his expert gaze taking in everything from his vantage point. The single, fatal shot had been fired from this room on the top floor of the Ritz-Carlton, approximately one kilometer from the parade grandstand. The room was neat, orderly, with no evidence anyone had even laid on the bed. A table had been pushed over to the window where a hole had been cut out, no doubt so the bullet's path wasn't interrupted.

It should have taken them hours, if not longer, to find this place, yet an anonymous tip had been called in from a lobby phone with a cryptic message.

"The albatross is now around your neck."

It meant nothing to him, but it also meant it wasn't an innocent bystander phoning in a tip about something they saw that they shouldn't have. Whoever made the call was involved.

He stared at the sniper rifle still set up on the table. American. An M24 Sniper Weapon System. Would they be so stupid to use their own weaponry, or was someone else framing the Americans? There was no way he could see the American government doing something so foolish, something that could lead to war. A spent shell casing sat on the table, which surprised him. Normally, snipers policed their brass, but then again, normally snipers left with their weapon.

His junior partner cleared his throat behind him. "Sir, I've got the names of the people who were checked into this room. They're Canadian."

Gridnev's eyebrow shot up at his partner's revelation. "Then we should be expecting an apology shortly."

Everyone in the room laughed.

"I assume they have them on camera when they checked in?"

His partner shook his head. "They didn't check in together, but they did check out together."

"They checked out?"

"Yes, sir. According to the desk clerk, they said they didn't like the view, so had decided to switch hotels."

"How did they leave?"

"They asked for a cab then made a phone call before leaving."

Curiouser and curiouser.

"So they phoned in the tip. They're acting as if they don't expect to be touched," muttered Gridnev.

"Then they're fools, sir. They just tried to kill our President. They think they can get away with it?"

Gridnev eyed the man. "Do you think that's what's happened here?"

"Of course. He was aiming for the President but missed, and instead hit the General."

Gridnev shook his head, waving his arm at the weapon and the setup. "A man like this doesn't miss, but if he does, he takes a second shot. No, the General was the target. The question is why, though that's a question for another day. Right now, the only thing we're focused on is capturing those responsible."

He stepped closer to the table and leaned forward, peering through the cut glass, revealing a clear line of sight to the grandstand. The room had been chosen for this very view, and the fact these people had checked out complaining about it was a further indication they were toying with them.

And it pissed him off.

He looked down at the spent shell casing sitting beside an unfired round, both atop a folded piece of hotel stationery. "Gloves," he said, holding his hand up. Someone rushed over and slapped a pair of latex gloves in his hand. He snapped them on then moved the rounds and lifted the paper. He unfolded it, surprised to see that it was written in flawless Russian.

Albatross is finished, or you're next.

His eyes narrowed. What the hell did albatross mean? And who was next?

Someone rushed into the room. "Sir, we've got them at the airport!"

He spun toward the new arrival. "We have them in custody?"

"No, sir. They're sitting at their departure gate. The commander on the ground is awaiting your instructions."

"Good. Keep them under observation. If they try to leave or board the airplane, arrest them. Otherwise, wait for my instructions." He strode from the room, fishing his phone from his pocket as he dialed the number of the man who had assigned him the investigation. It was answered immediately. "Sir, we've got them at the airport. We can take them down at any time, but there's something you need to know first. The shooter left a message with the spent shell casing and a fresh bullet sitting on top of it."

"What does it say?"

"It says, in Russian, 'Albatross is finished, or you're next.' Sir, what does it mean, what is albatross?"

"Stand by."

Dead air filled his ear then there was a click. "Do you recognize my voice?"

Gridnev froze, his heart hammering as his entire body broke out in a cold sweat. He reached for the wall to steady himself, for he did indeed recognize the voice. "Y-yes, sir."

"This is what I want you to do."

Sheremetyevo Alexander S. Pushkin International Airport
Moscow, Russia

"There's another one. Two o'clock."

Kane sat beside Sherrie at gate D-32. He directed his gaze slightly to his right, spotting the new arrival. "That makes six."

"I think you're forgetting about the other twenty."

Kane shook his head. "No, those are all uniformed. They're at every gate because of the lockdown. These six are here just for us."

"And you still think this was a good idea?"

"Yes. It's the only way to know for sure if the message was received."

"Wouldn't the fact the attacks stopped be all the confirmation we'd need?"

Kane leaned back and put his arm around her, still in character. "Maybe this time. But what about next time? We delivered a message today. We told him to never do it again. We have to know if they agree, and what happens in the next few minutes will tell us."

He glanced over at the large display showing all the flights canceled. The moment they were finished at the hotel room, they had checked out with an excuse that would be so memorable that when questioned, the desk clerk would tell the investigators exactly what Kane wanted them to hear. They had taken a regular cab to the airport, and had arrived just as the flights were canceled. No one was allowed to leave, but they were letting people in, probably under the hopes the assassin would attempt to escape by air. It was a reasonable hope. After all, most assassins didn't leave a clear trail behind them. They would come here and simply wait for the authorities to do whatever they were going to before reopening the airport.

But with half a dozen plainclothes officers now surrounding their gate, it was clear the Russians had received the message and followed the obvious clues. He and Sherrie were unarmed, and there would be no point in fighting if they were arrested. If they were, typically they would be disavowed, and the government would claim they were acting on their own. He wondered what Washington would do this time. The message had to be delivered. Would the American government stand behind them and say it was retaliation for what the Russians had done, perhaps claim that General Utkin was behind everything, and they trust that the Russian president was in the dark? Yet none of that mattered, for he was convinced his plan would work.

Cheers erupted throughout the terminal as the boards updated, all the flight statuses changed. The soldiers slowly receded into the background, and everyone seated around them eagerly stared at the staff at the check-in counter for any indication they were about to board.

"Ten o'clock," whispered Sherrie.

Kane glanced over at a man in a poorly tailored suit that failed to conceal his shoulder holster. "This is it."

The man wasn't happy, the thin smile forced as he sat beside Kane. An announcement was made, indicating their flight would begin boarding, and those around them sprang to their feet.

"Well, I guess that's us," said Kane as he rose.

The man held out his left arm, slightly blocking him.

"If you would wait a moment, it would be appreciated."

This *was* it. The question was whether this man was waiting for the innocent to vacate the area before they were taken down, or was he merely waiting for a little more privacy. As the passengers were quickly processed through the gate, the half-dozen plainclothesmen that had arrived earlier closed in, no longer attempting to blend, forcing Kane to reassess what might be about to happen.

As the last of the passengers disappeared through the doors to the jetway, the man finally spoke, staring directly ahead. "I've been asked to give you a message."

Kane's heart couldn't help but race. "And that is?"

"The albatross is dead."

Kane suppressed a sigh. "Then I assume our business is done."

The man rose then stared down at them. "You and your friend are free to go."

Kane rose, as did Sherrie. He extended a hand and the man took it. "Until next time?"

The man glared at him, clearly not pleased with the situation. "Don't push your luck." The man let go of Kane's hand, then turned on his heel and walked briskly away, the other agents following.

Sherrie breathed a heavy sigh. "Well, that didn't go the way I expected."

Kane chuckled as they headed toward the gate. "You should really know by now that I'm always right."

She gave him a look. "You and I both know that's bullshit. You're wrong plenty of times. It's just that in the end, things always seem to work out for you."

They showed their boarding passes and passports, then were ushered through, the staff clearly nervous, having just witnessed the exchange. The doors of the jetway were closed behind them, and as they stepped onto the plane and took their seats, he smiled with the knowledge that not only had his message been sent and received, it had been accepted. The Russians would think twice before targeting American soldiers.

Otherwise, America might be forced to send its messenger once again.

Sarwani Residence
Kabul, Afghanistan

Mo sat cross-legged, puffing on his hookah pipe, still decompressing from his brief mission with Kane as he gripped his phone in his spare hand. Part of him wanted it to ring with Kane on the other end telling him he had to evac because they were leaving. But another part wanted it to remain silent, for it would mean they were safe, that no one was after them.

Yet they weren't safe.

Even if that phone didn't ring, it was just a matter of time. So many people like him would soon be dead. He was certain of it, as were others he had spoken to that worked for the Americans and their NATO allies. The moment the government fell, they were targets.

He couldn't understand why the promises made hadn't been kept. Fortunately, he had saved most of the money he had been paid, the amounts generous when compared to the average Afghan income. If need be, it should be enough to get them across the border, but he had to make those arrangements himself, and he didn't know where to begin.

His wife walked into the room, a smile on her face as she hummed a lullaby she loved to sing to their children. She paused. "What's troubling my husband?"

He forced a smile. "Nothing."

She motioned toward the cellphone. "Are you expecting a call?"

He grunted. "Not so much expecting as wishing for."

She frowned. "For the Americans to call?" She harrumphed. "You would think that after everything you've done for them, they would keep their promise."

"I'm sure it's complicated," he said. "I have no doubt—" The phone vibrated in his hand with a text message, and he nearly soiled himself. He checked the display.

Five minutes.

He gulped then scrambled to his feet.

"What is it?" asked his wife as he rushed into their bedroom.

"We're leaving in five minutes. Ready the children."

"What?"

"You heard me. Five minutes!"

"Ready them for what?"

"We're leaving the house. Permanently." She followed him into the bedroom as his heart raced with fear and joy. He grabbed her by both arms. "The Americans. They're coming for us!" She jumped for joy then gave him a quick hug. He pushed her away. "Get the children, now. Four minutes!"

He grabbed the bags he had prepared for them the moment he had got home from the mission, tossing them onto the bed. He took one last look around the room. There were things he would take if he had time, if he had room, all memories of the difficult life he had shared with his wife and family. His heart sickened at the thought they were about to leave without saying goodbye to their family and friends, though once in America, once he gained his citizenship, perhaps he could gain their freedom as well.

He checked his phone. Two minutes. He gathered up the bags and headed for the front door, dropping them in front of it as the children scrambled to put on their sandals and his wife carefully fit her chador in place, making certain no hair was visible. The sound of vehicles pulling up outside was followed almost immediately by three quick raps on the door. He opened it to find an American lieutenant and several soldiers with him.

"Mr. Mohammed Sarwani?"

Mo nodded.

"I'm here to take you and your family into protective custody. Are you ready to go?"

"Yes, sir."

"Very well. I'll ask you to hurry."

Mo stepped outside to see two Humvees, one with the rear door open, a sergeant beckoning them toward it. He urged the children forward, his wife following, herding them like sheep. He stepped back inside and grabbed their bags, taking one last look at his home of so many years, and at a life he would never see again, men like him no longer welcome in their own country.

And as he closed the door for the last time, he prayed to Allah that he and his family would be welcome in their new country, and that his wife and children would finally find peace now that a promise had been kept.

THE END

ACKNOWLEDGMENTS

When I first read about the Russian bounty program to target American soldiers in Afghanistan, I was as outraged as anyone. And a little skeptical. Though as more evidence came out, including testimony that payouts could be as high as $100,000 a head depending on the seniority of the soldier killed, my doubts waned. Yet you have to consider who would be behind it.

Russia today is far more powerful than the Soviet Union, not due to military might, but through economic power and the impunity under which it can now operate. This pretender democracy, whom only the most naïve would claim their leader is legitimately elected, charges around the world stage, assassinating rivals, backing dictatorships, supplying insurgencies, and invading sovereign countries.

Why not a bounty program that targeted Americans?

Every single action Russia has taken over the past decade has gone unanswered, beyond rhetoric. Russia's oil and natural gas are simply too important to Europe. America has lost interest with the Cold War "won," and a generation has no idea the horrors the Soviet Union committed. Most in the West are content to sit behind their screens and ignore the fact that we are entering into or are already in Cold War 2.0, because of the distinction that no one worries about Russia invading Western Europe or North America. And while that might be true, can we allow a country to assassinate people on our own soil simply because they spoke out against the leadership? Russia is out of control, and the world once again needs to make a stand.

A message needs to be sent.

But not by me. I'm a lover not a fighter.

I often take little tidbits from my life and throw them into my books, and this one is no different. I remember when I was in Moscow, staring through the scope of my—wait, I forgot, I'm a lover not a fighter. What was the little anecdote from my life?

BD's Renault "Le Car" story.

I miss that car, and I'd take it over my Jag any day.

As usual, there are people to thank. My dad for all the research, Ian Kennedy for some terminology info, and Brent Richards for some weapons info, and, as always, my wife, daughter, my late mother who will always be an angel on my shoulder as I write, as well as my friends for their continued support, and my fantastic proofreading team! Also, a special thanks to these followers on my Facebook page who helped name some of the characters: Sam Koski, Becca Salinas Franco, Don Woodie, and William Mauk, as well as Jon Fraser for picking Spock's new ride and Chris Kalle for some Aussie insight.

To those who have not already done so, please visit my website at www.jrobertkennedy.com, then sign up for the Insider's Club to be notified of new book releases. Your email address will never be shared or sold.

Thank you once again for reading.

CPSIA information can be obtained
at www.ICGtesting.com
Printed in the USA
LVHW030950060423
743660LV00009B/28

9 781990 418570